Rebirth

The man was tired and bored. Perhaps the first came from the second. In any event, he was the most fortunate of men: anything he desired was there for the taking, available at the touch of a button, the call of an order.

But . . . he desired nothing.

He owned everything, but wanted only to stop. He needed nothing, but searched for the secret that would put an end to his boredom.

Then came the call for action, the request for a return to duty, and he took it eagerly. Perhaps this was the way back to life. It's depressing to be an immortal. . . .

STAR ROGUE
is for
Michelle Malkin,
Debbie Kogan,
Ron Stoloff,
and
Kathy Surgenor.

STAR ROGUE

Lin Carter

WILDSIDE PRESS

www.wildsidepress.com

STAR ROGUE

EXCERPTS

"In popular folklore, as differentiated from the formal science of historiography, we encounter a 'para-reality' which more than compensates in color and variety for what it lacks in a soberly factual basis. Probably the most intriguing of all the imaginative detail folklore has added as embroidery to the margins of historiography is the concept that, behind the scenes and unknown to us all, the flow of historical events is secretly being manipulated by a super-cabal of telepaths and masterminds known only by the code name of *Citadel*. Why these mahatmas of mystery, this secret brotherhood of idealistic supermen (controlled since the very founding of the Great Imperium by an undying being most appropriately known as 'the Eternal'), should bother themselves with the secret mastery of the galaxy—much less *how* they do it—is, oddly enough, not explained by the inventive imaginations of popular folklore. The sober consensus of all serious historians, to which the present writer most emphatically subscribes, is that we can safely relegate the wonder-working masterminds of the Citadel to the marvelous regions of sheer myth and fable, along with the Space Hag, the Rim ghosts, and the trans-dimensional migrations of the Vokanna,

5

fleeing down the ages from their peculiar, nameless, pursuing doom. For the simple fact remains that if any such super-cabal of supermen *were* controlling the dynamics of history, we should see the signs of it in every age."

—HERIAN, Lord Altair: *Notes Towards a Science of History*, reel one. Published by Bradis Recordings, Meridian, The Hub; Year 1187 of the Imperium.

"The fact of the matter is, simply, that the concept of the Eternal is merely the most recent development in a very old continuum of folk-belief. From the very earliest days of the interstellar age folklore has recorded fables of this kind, from the so-called 'Wandering Spaceman' of early Centaurian literature to that long-lived adventurer of the spaceway, 'Long Tom.' All of this probably stems from speculations among the under-educated early colonials stimulated by contact with extra-terrestrial races of considerable longevity such as the familiar Boygyar of Tau Ceti. The sequence of thought doubtless went along the lines of: if a Boyg lives a natural life-span of about four thousand Standard years, maybe a hominid can do the same—and so on. My point is, however, that the notion of an immortal being of Earth lineage and heroic stature is certainly far from new, and very far from being an original component of the sequence of myths centering about the fabulous Citadel. Even in the remote era of the United Systems we read of legendary 'Saul Everest, Earth's only immortal man,' heroic secret mastermind of that ancient government who was destroyed by the rise of Nordonn but who somehow circumvented death to reappear, born anew out of the very crucible of

6

the race, in the early days of the First Imperium. And today we have those puppet masters of history, the secret supermen of the Citadel, and their mysterious captain, the Eternal. The dreams of Man remain the same in every age.

"The unfortunate truth, however, is that hominid man is crucified to the hands of a physiological clock, by which his days are inexorably measured. While advances in nutritional science, geriatric medicine and experiments in controlled genetics have enabled the race to attain a far greater life-expectancy than that enjoyed by the citizens of earlier times, cellular tissue remains mortal, fatigue acids accumulate insidiously, and immortals such as the Eternal of legend remain simply that: a legend, no more."

—CHOS'F L. GAMMOND, Ch. D.: *Gene Surgery, Longevity, and Human Life* (Intro., xvii). Published by The Beldris Imperia School of Hominid Medicine, Cassini III, Central Orion, Carina-Cygnus; Year 3904 of the Imperium.

ONE

I was out riding in the hills when the call came. That's why I didn't receive it. Maybe I should have had a phone with me, but you get out of the habit of wearing one after awhile. Since no one in the galaxy knew where I was living—or even that I was still alive—a personal phone seemed like a useless ornament to carry around. And it had been at least a century since anything had come up that was urgent enough for one of my monitors to call me directly.

It was a perfect spring morning. The hills above the house were a mass of yellow poplar, hickory, and mountain laurel, thick with bright new buds the color of chartreuse. Robins were frisking about and there were young rabbits in the field. It was one of those days when it was just too beautiful outdoors to stay inside.

When I had Home terraformed, I settled on a Connecticut ecology because that was the most beautiful country I had ever seen. I mean the *old* Connecticut, of course, back before the days of the mile-high megacities and twenty-five-lane robot expressways. Way back when it was green and lovely in a way no one alive today but myself could remember. . .

So I started out right after breakfast, told the house to mind the dogs, saddled up Sultan and headed out over the fields. Jewels of dew glittered on the ferns and field mice scampered from under his heavy hooves. We skirted the edge of the woods for a while, going nowhere in particular, just liking

9

the fresh clean smell of dew and sweet grass and the piny tang of the woods. I relaxed and enjoyed the surge of the great horse under me. One glimpse of Sultan would have thrilled the soul of any paleontologist specializing in pre-Imperium Centaurus Sector lifeforms. He was a coal-black thoroughbred, four years old and full of the devil. I suppose he was the last true horse alive; the species is believed to have been extinct for three thousand years or so. As a matter of fact, it is—except for Sultan. And the future Sultans I keep under stasis in the sperm tanks.

After a while we turned into the woods. They were oak and chestnut, hickory and pine, mostly. Last winter's leaves were turning into mulch underfoot and Sultan snorted and tossed his head at the rank odor of decay that rose as his hooves disturbed the top layers. Rabbits and squirrels scuttled in the underbrush and a bluejay squawked from somewhere above us. We went through the dark green twilight for a time and then took the trail that led to the shore. Sultan's sire and grandsire and great-grandsire had made that trail. He shied just once, as something crossed the path ahead of us. It was too dark under the trees to see for sure, but from the spicy, musky smell I think it was fat skunk waddling about on his skunkish business.

We came back by way of the seashore. The tide was out and the gulls were busy feeding and quarrelling over the tiny shellfish swept in and then abandoned on the slick wet gray sand by the retreating waves.

When we got to the shore I let Sultan go because I knew he felt like stretching his legs. He was happy with the freedom and frisked like a colt. Then he laid his ears back, stretched out his nose and galloped for all he was worth. The gulls exploded squawking in a startled cloud as we came rocketing down the wet sandy shore, scattering clods behind us. I squinted my eyes half-shut against the wind of our rush and tasted the salt spray on my lips.

The sea, to my left hand, was a gray, choppy mirror, bright and burnished by the sun. I am very proud of my sea. And of my sun, for that matter. When you consider that, in the beginning, Home was just a raw hunk of naked airless rock, you can imagine what a bitch it was to terraform. It's only about 500 kilometers in diameter, which makes it smaller than Outpost, or Way Station, or Ceres back in the Sol system. Being so small meant the engineers had to build everything in special: an artificial gravity field set at Earth norm, a tailor-made atmosphere, a complete ecology—the works, as we used to say. It *was* quite a job. You should see the engines that make my tides, for instance.

Or take my sun. We couldn't very well transpose a body of stellar mass into paraspace, not at 42 cpu's per metric slug, we couldn't. To say nothing of a *real* sun; think of the problems of compensating for the difference in energy levels!

So I settled for a closed energy field, locked it around the asteroid and worked out a sort of Phoenix effect that makes the outer shell fluoresce way up in the visual octaves. It sheds a respectable amount of light, and you can get a sunburn if you stay outside all day, working with your japon off and torso bare. But it's not enough to heat Home, of course. For that, we planted fusion engines in the core; for that, and to power the gravity field. The whole job cost a fortune (a half dozen fortunes, really) but, damn it all, I wanted me a *sun!* Or a reasonable facsimile, at least.

After we had scared all the seagulls and stretched

our legs a little, we headed for the house. It's up in the valley above the seashore with the hills behind it and the woods beyond. Since there's only me, not counting the dogs and Sultan, most of Home is woods and fields. My sea is really only a big lake. But it *is* salt water, and it *does* have tides.

I built the house myself. With a little robotic assistance, of course. I built it just the way I wanted it, long and low and rambling, all redwood logs and rough fieldstone and a real slate roof. The living room, as we used to call it, has hand-hewn exposed beams in the ceiling and a fieldstone fireplace so big you can sit in it. A lot of the house is built underground—lab facilities, vaults, files, stores and the workshops, to say nothing of the main thedomin installation. Only the living area is above ground. *Wanderer*'s hangar is in the back. It looks like a big red barn, and it is, as he shares it with Sultan.

When we came up into the yard the dogs came out to welcome us, tails wagging and tongues lolling. My big St. Bernard and one of the little dachshunds had started out that morning with Sultan and I but the house knew better and turned them back at the pasture gate. Now both dachsies danced around Sultan yapping hysterically. My big boy woofed in his deep voice and wagged his huge plume of a tail. Even the puppies came toddling out from their favorite napping-place under the wild rose bushes to see what was going on. They got underfoot, as is the way with puppies, but Sultan stepped carefully through them with delicate, precise steps bending low to watch his footing. The yapping dachsies were beneath his dignity to notice but he gave the pups a curious sniff and licked one from stumpy nose to small tail as he went through the crowd.

As I climbed out of the saddle, the house cleared its throat and said: "There has been a call from Monitor R-2. Received and recorded at 10:19."

I stood there holding on to the saddle horn and felt a tingle go chasing itself up and down my spine. As I said before, it had been a good century since the last time I'd had a call. The monitors are set to make a direct call only in case something big comes up. Something like invasion, war, revolution, the assassination of a regnant Imperator, the collapse of a dynasty or the energy-death of the universe. So this must be a *big* one.

I told the house okay but, urgent call or no urgent call, I had my obligation to Sultan to take care of first. I took him into the barn he shares with *Wanderer*, unsaddled him, rubbed him down, gave him mashed bran and fresh water and told him he was a good fella. Then I went in and listened to the playback. The dogs followed me in, all except the pups, who had fallen asleep under the rose bushes again. I listened to the playback. Twice.

It *was* serious. Or it might be serious. It was, at any rate, damn odd. Odd enough for the monitor to make the decision to place a direct call to Home. Most routine monthly reports from my monitor system are received by the house thedomin, which digests them and gives me a printed rundown. Rarely is there anything so urgent as to demand my immediate attention. After all, I retired a century and a half ago and I mean to stay retired. I like to keep in touch with what's going on but I leave it up to Citadel to handle emergencies. I wondered if Citadel knew about *this* one. . . .

I mulled it over while the house made my lunch and I used the 'fresher. Then I stretched out in the big

13

pneumo in the living room, wolfed down my lunch and whittled away at a large brandy. I was still thinking about it when the snifter was empty.

The message that had caused all this trouble was a deleocast from Monitor R-2. The R-prefix denoted it as one of the Rim series but I had frankly forgotten just what the Rim series had been established for in the first place. The house refreshed my memory on this.

I do not mean to give the impression that I am absent-minded. Just—practical. You see, when you've lived as long as I have, you accumulate quite a load of memories and some of them are superfluous.

Let me illustrate this with an example drawn from ancient history. I remember an old "movie"—an obsolete artform, a sort of recorded visual drama. It was a comedy about a stodgy scholar with a phenomenal memory of encyclopedic dimensions. He decided to cash in on his skill by appearing on a "quiz show"— an organized competition with large monetary prizes given for the best memory which used to be conducted as a species of entertainment, so-called. He was about to walk away with a fortune when they stopped him cold with the final query. They had asked him the one question he could not answer—to recite his social security number! We would call it his Citizen's Code today, but the principle remains the same. Even way back then, every citizen walked around with long strings of identifying numerals attached to his name and who could be bothered storing all that data?

It's like that with an ordinary lifetime's load of casual memory accumulation. Live long enough, and you end up with a real shortage of storage space.

So you see, an immortal has his problems, too.

I can't be bothered remembering such routine data,

so I let the house file it away for me. This is not to say I have a bad memory, because I have a superb information-storage-and-retrieval system up there in the mnemonic lattice of my cerebral cortex; an immortal *has* to develop a well-organized memory or go blooey from sheer cumulative overload. But the house has a better brain than even I do, so I let it take care of the routine details.

Of course, a thedomin isn't really much like a human brain but the comparison is close enough. The kind of A-prime thedomin that runs my house and my cruiser is an artificial intelligence capable of handling a virtually infinite number of information-bits simultaneously. "Infinite" may be too strong a term but the house thedomin can actually store on tap for instant recall something like 100^{20} data-bits. Now *that's* what I call a filing system! And if its capacities are not quite "infinite," they're certainly close enough to make the difference neglible.

The thedomin is a great tool. It has freed half the race from routine work and liberated the human intelligence for more important tasks. A thedomin's great-great-great grandad about two thousand times removed was an old-fashioned IBM computer, but the equivalence is brutally unfair. It bears about the same relation to a primitive computer as Chernikov does to a caveman.

But I am digressing all over space . . . I never played with autobiography before, and I'm not at all sure why I am yakking away at it now, since I plan to make damn sure no one will ever hear this cassette.

Anyway, the house informed me that I set up the Rim series to conduct longterm studies of fluctuations in the galactic magnetic field. This was back over two centuries ago, when I was planning to retire. At the time I was in the middle of a research program on paramagnetic wave patterns. Like the five hundred-or-so other monitor stations I set up around the galaxy—my private, personal watchdog system—the Rim series consisted of thedomin-controlled secret research satellites powered with "eternity" ion-exchange batteries, shielded from chance discovery by light-baffles, tucked away in asdarproof vacuoles, and locked in neutrino-retaining bentspace fields. They are going to run forever unless commanded to self-destruct.

Now, it seems that Monitor R-2 is positioned in the fringe of the outermost of the Range Stars. The 300-odd stars in the Range group lie at the further extremity of the middle arm of our galactic spirial, which still retains its old, prespace-travel appellation of Carina-Cygnus. The Range Stars, which to this day are sparsely populated, mostly rural agricultural or "suburban" planetary systems, are the end, the jumping-off place. There's nothing beyond them, nothing at all, but the black and empty sea of intergalactic space . . . all the way to our two nearest neighbors, the Magellanic Clouds. The lonely Range Stars wink and glitter at the galactic Rim like outpost beacons on the shore of a dark, unknown, and unsailed sea.

Since concluding my study of paramagnetics I hadn't paid any attention to the R-series monitor reports. Most of my monitors perform simple tasks like charting the rise and fall of Chernikov radiation, take periodic mu/lambda particle counts, and graph out novae data. More than half the monitors in my private information-gathering system listen in to newscasts, digest the data and feed the digest to Home on deleo tightbeam.

But a thedomin, even an "idiot-level" thedomin

16

like my Rim series of monitors, is intelligent enough to be able to make value judgments on the data they collect, process and forward. And R-2 figured its data was important enough for a direct call to the boss. I wondered. It just might be right. . . .

For the rest of the day I just puttered around. I have eight or nine study projects going on currently. At the moment I am mastering spoken Sanskrit, learning to read the Sirius II petroglyphs at sight, boning up on the last decade's accomplishments in plenum mechanics, rereading the Silver poets, and trying to invent an absolutely unbreakable code, i.e., a synthetic language with a working vocabulary of 10,000 words coined at pure random. And, among other things, I am playing with this experiment in autobiography. If I don't get bored with it, I may turn out a full set of memoirs, of which this cassette would be about #74.

Does this hobby program sound self-contradictory, considering what I was saying just a moment ago about not wanting to clutter up my mnemonic lattice with superfluous memories? If so, I'm sorry, but I have as much right to be inconsistent as you do.

The thing is this: while an immortal does tend to eliminate the tiresome chore of remembering routine data, he also soon learns that he has to keep his mind supple and flexible or it ossifies into habit-patterns which turn out to be detrimental in the long run. What I mean is—boredom sets in, and that can be deadly. Now an immortal is far more prone to boredom than a short-lifer. You may find Henggren's *Moons of Saturn* enthralling and inexhaustible but take it from me, the 500,000th time you play that particular neosymphony it has nothing left of itself to reveal to you. And if your musical tastes are limited to the Third Imperium neosymphonic school of composers alone, you have reached a dead-end as far as music is concerned.

An immortal's life is filled with dead-ends. Best you learn to avoid them by a continuing program of exploring new interests. The mind is very much like a muscle in many ways. Keep it occupied with new and different exercises, and you keep it limber and supple, alive and healthy. Keep using it in the same old ways, and it atrophies in the long run.

But here I am digressing again!

So, anyway, I played and puttered the rest of the day away, but I'm afraid my heart just wasn't in it—which is another way of saying my mind was elsewhere. To be exact, it was out there on the Rim wondering just what the hell that enigmatic report from monitor R-2 really implied.

A little later on, the house whipped up a superb dinner, and, over coffee (yes, *real* coffee: like the house, the beverage is extinct, except here on Home) and liqueurs, I listened with only half an ear to some recorded verse—my nightly canto of Radelix's Morgantyr Epic. I went to bed early.

But not to sleep.

That message kept going through the empty space between my ears—which I laughingly call my brain. What did it mean? What *could* it mean? How important was it? How important *might* it be?

I must have tossed and turned, trying to get to sleep. Because the dogs sensed something was wrong. The big St. Bernard, who sleeps at the left side of the bed, stood up, whined deep in his throat and laid his huge paw gently on my arm questioningly. I rubbed my fingers through the thick ruff of fur on his neck and told him that he was a good boy and that it was all right and to go to sleep now. He lay down with a heavy sigh and slept. His mind was at rest. But mine was not. I couldn't turn it off.

Here was the reason why.

The galaxy's magnetic field fluctuates according to a complex rhythm for reasons of its own. But R-2 for the past six months had been taking readings on an enormous disturbance in the field. The center of this disturbance was cruising along the Rim in a certain direction and at a fixed speed.

What was causing it?

According to the magnetigraphs, it was an object of almost stellar—certainly planetary—mass. A ship of any conceivable size, even an armada, would not register a fraction of that mass.

Now, it could be a rogue star. A wanderer from the far places. Rogue stars, rogue planets, bodies dislodged somehow from their accustomed coigns and orbits—although as rare as scales on a Pterian, had been known for a good ten thousand years.

But the house had already cross-referenced its memory of recent astrophysical news. A rogue star wandering the Rim would have made the news, for the occurrence was unusual. No such news had been announced on the deleocasts in the past six months—in the past year, for that matter.

A dark star? A burn-out cinder, wandering from the Beyond? Perhaps. Such a body would not necessarily have shown up on visual sightings or on photogramic sightings, although asdar surveys would have spotted it without trouble.

Maybe. Just maybe.

But what was keeping me from sleep was another memory-bit. This was the twenty-seventh year of the Empery of Kermian XIX of the House of the Tregephontanes, or A.D. 7-177 if you prefer the Old Style. The Eighth Imperium. In the four thousand one hundred and fourteen years since The Divine Arion founded the House of Baracheus, vast portions of the first galaxy had been explored, colonized, civilized and tamed.

We were almost ready to take the Big Jump—the mightiest voyage across space ever attempted—the history-making first venture into a neighboring galaxy. And the nearest of our neighbors in galactic space were the Greater and the Lesser Magellanic Clouds. For a century or more Imperial scientists had studied the problems entailed in such a colossal attempt. For to open up another galaxy, even a small one like the G.M.C., *is* colossal. Think of the man-power needed for such a project. Think of the *varieties* of man-power—hundreds of sciences were involved. You would need pilots, galactographers, linguists, communications experts, engineers, planetographers, telepathicists, diplomats, government representatives, diovonicists, doctors, naval personnel, tacticians, biologists, ecologists, and just about every other kind of ologist you could think of.

The preliminary survey personnel, in fact, has been estimated—conservatively—at two hundred million specialists.

Now, no one ship, no one fleet, can be expected to carry so many people so far for so long a trip. So the Imperium (with a few carefully timed and placed nudges from Citadel) came up with the answer, eventually. Such a ship does in fact exist that can carry 200,000,000 people through space—not just for a century but for millennia. In fact, we have a lot of ships around that can do it.

They are called . . . *planets.*

In other words, stock up an Earth-type planet with two hundred million specialists dislodge the planet and its sun from orbit and aim them at the shores of

the Magellanics. In time, they'll get there intact—
they or their children.

For the past twenty years they've been doing in-
tensive study of the problems of launching and main-
taining a "mobile planet system," as the deleocasters
have labelled it. One of the Range Stars will be picked
—several have volunteered. It may be Segemon or
Cavalaris or Ordovoy. And in another twenty years
they may be ready to do it, and the Big Jump will be
launched.

So . . . isn't it a peculiar coincidence that something of planetary or even stellar mass is drifting
around the fringes of the galaxy right now . . . drifting *just beyond* the outermost of the Range Stars
themselves?

It makes you stop and think, doesn't it?

Like—maybe the Magellanics have beaten us to it?

That's what was keeping me awake. And I had a
hunch I wouldn't be getting much sleep until I found
out just What was cruising the shores of space out
there.

Or just Who.

TWO

So, bright and early the next morning I set out on another little trip. But not on horseback, this time. I went out to the barn, "woke up" *Wanderer*, gave him a set of coordinates to chew over, and told him to get ready.

I had come to a decision there in what somebody— obviously another sufferer-from-insomnia—had once very aptly called "the stilly watches of the night." Namely, that I was going to have to check on this one myself.

Oh, sure, I had retired all right. But that didn't mean I couldn't take a little vacation cruise once in a while. I could leave Home to take care of itself. The house was perfectly capable of watching over the dogs, seeing they got fed on time, keeping them out of mischief and out of fights, or even giving them a little medical attention if they did get into fights—anything up to and including major surgery. And the house could feed and water and even exercise Sultan, too. There was nothing keeping me here if I wanted to go.

And, sure, I could have called the magnetic field fluctuations to the attention of Citadel if I wanted to and left it to them to investigate. But—Citadel didn't know where I was, or even that I was still living. I planned it that way when I turned command over to Ben Dalmers, my longtime adjutant. If they knew where they could get hold of me, Citadel would be phoning me every time the Heir of Tregephon had a toothache. I had trained Citadel to make its own decisions and to get along without me. By now, who-ever was running things probably thought I was as extinct as Nordonn, the horse, or coffee. And I wanted to keep it that way.

So I couldn't pass the buck to Acting Colonel Dal-mers, of whoever was running the show these days. Why should I blow my cover (as we used to say, way back when) over something that probably wasn't a nine-sector emergency after all, but just a dark star gone rogue?

So I was going to check out this one myself. Chances are, there wasn't much in it. But I felt like a little action and somebody had to get the answers to this question. And that somebody was going to be me.

But first things first. I had learned a little in my old age. Time was when I would have gone charging off to the Range Stars without a moment's thought, and without even knowing what I was looking for. I de-cided to play this one smart.

I checked with the house thedomin's memory and discovered that galactic astronomers interested in the study of the Rim are organized into a Rim Star As-tronomical Association whose central headquarters and, more importantly, central files are located on Demaratus in Quadrant One. That was the logical place to start.

Demaratus, otherwise known as Beta Cygni IV, was in the second galactic arm, which is still known by its ancient name of Carina-Cygnus. That was to be my first stop. So I gave *Wanderer* the coordinates, put the house on full control, said goodby to the dogs, and started out.

One reason I have such privacy is that after we terraformed Home, we transposed it into paraspace. Paraspace is a name the plenumographers thought up to describe the aborted semicosmos that interconnects with our own on a slightly lower ATS modulation. Paraspace is a universe that never quite got started. It comes in handy because in paraspace the Newtonian laws of motion, the Einsteinian laws of relativity and the Chernikovian laws of subspectrum radiation all operate a little differently from how they function in normal space/time. In paraspace, for example, the speed of light is not the top velocity limit it is in normal space. Several forms of radiation and matter itself, in its mu/lambda state of transposition, can move a lot faster than even light does in normal space. Hence we use paraspace for transportation. And for communications, of course. Deleo waves propagate at the usual c speed in normal space. In paraspace, they move so fast that communications are almost instantaneous, even from one edge of the galaxy to the other.

I'm not going to try to explain how a deleo transmission can travel so much faster than light as to be all but simultaneous. For one thing, it would take me about fifteen pages of equations to do it. For another thing, even the Chernikov theoreticians themselves admit they don't quite know how it works. And, anyway, I was talking about Home, and privacy.

The thing is, as I said a minute ago, paraspace is a universe that aborted in embryo, so to speak. The way its physical laws are all mucked up makes this no great surprise. But one odd thing about paraspace—is no matter exists in it. None at all. Not so much as a single lonely little molecule bopping around by itself.

Which means that when a ship transposes into mu/lambda phase to make a long trip short, it doesn't bother opening the irises for a look at the scenery because there isn't anything to see. And it doesn't bother probing about with an asdar field to avoid random meteors because there ain't none. It just turns the steering over to the ship thedomin and off it goes.

Since Home is the only chunk of solid matter in the whole of paraspace, and well off the travel routes, it isn't about to be spotted—even if anybody was looking for it, which they aren't because nobody but me knows it's there in the first place. And even if somebody *was* looking for it they'd have a mighty hard time finding it, since paraspace is just as big as the normal space/time universe, only darker and emptier.

Hmm. I seem to have a few things yet to learn about autobiographicology, if there is such a word which I know there isn't as I just made it up. I started out trying to explain why, when *Wanderer* made his lift off Home, we didn't have to make transposition into paraspace. Because we were already there being the reason. Instead I digressed like crazy. Does every autobiographer run off at the mouth with a mike in his hand, I wonder? Or is it just me? It's probably a very good thing no one but me will ever slap this cassette into the player and expose his brain to my rambling, disconnected and deplorably conversational style . . .

Which reminds me, I had better explain before I go too much further why I habitually refer to *Wanderer* by the masculine pronoun—in shocking violation of sacroscanct naval tradition, which says that all ships are to be referred to as "she." You just don't live as long as I have without developing a healthy contempt for the dead hand of Custom and Tradition. But the simple fact is that I "awoke" the *Wanderer* thedomin, and I educated it, and it speaks with a variant of my own voice. Now, it is common knowledge among thedominic psychoticists today, as it was among computer programmers ages ago, that if one person awakens and educates an artificial intelligence such as a thedomin (or even the old-fashioned computers which

26

were hardly more than super-adding-machines) something of that person's personality gets into the thinking processes of the machine. I am male and *Wanderer* just naturally "thinks masculinely." Hence my use of the masculine pronoun. Then again, I'd feel kind of silly calling something "she" that answers me in a deep baritone voder!

Anyway, it took *Wanderer* about one hour, Standard, to get from Home to the approximate vicinity of Demaratus in paraspace. That's damn good time, actually, but nonetheless I'm always amused by the dichotomy between paraspacial travel and deleo transmission. A solid object such as my ship, which has drive systems of my own design, ultimately based on secret—and superior—Citadel drive technology, and which can run rings around even the swiftest Courier boat or Naval scoutcraft, *still* can't push very far into what the experts call "the Chernikov Barrier." Even in paraspace, there is a top limit to velocity. It took me a good solid hour to get to Demaratus but if I had just sat on my lazy duff back on Home and *called*, the deleo beam would have travelled the same distance in a trifle under one hundredth of a second.

It's ironic. Maybe someday we'll be able to put our faces where our voices are—and just about as fast. But the way things stand in this enlightened twenty-seventh year of Kermian XIX, we can push a ship up to the norm-space equivalent of around 20 lights per second, but nothing more.

I was taking a nap when we decelerated towards the locale of Demaratus. *Wanderer* awoke me with a mental call—yes, the *Wanderer* is one of the few ships capable of thedomin-to-human telepathic communication.

I awoke, got the message and ordered a mug of hot coffee from *Wanderer's* autochef. Before I permitted

Wanderer to transpose into normal space and to start maneuvering into a parking orbit near the spacedock, I had a few basic safety precautions and procedures to unlimber.

Way back in the good old days when I was running Citadel, we had to operate undercover and with all kinds of security precautions. Because Citadel itself, and just about everything that Citadel did, was illegal as hell.

And it goes without saying that the above is, to this day, still true of Citadel and its activities. It is now and has been for more than four thousand years a secret underground organization. Citadel was created in the first place for self-protection . . . but that's another story, and a long one, and I'm not going to go into it at this time. To all intents and purposes, you can say that Citadel was set up to keep a close watch on the Imperium and to see that no one Imperator or regnant Imperia goes monomaniac and starts turning into a modern-day equivalent of Caligula, Hitler, Li Pao, the Second Prophet, or Nordonn I, which is the innate nature of empires in general and emperors in particular ("Power tends to corrupt" . . . etc., if you know your Lord Acton).

Of course, I no longer run Citadel. Nor am I, in point of fact, a member of Citadel in any capacity. However, this does not exactly give me carte blanche to zap about where and how I will, since I am *personally* illegal. That is, I am not a coded Citizen, being an immortal. Since I prize my own privacy and want to keep my natural-born longevity a secret, the Imperium doesn't even know I exist. And I want to keep things that way, which means I have to take Precautions.

The Precautions took about one Standard plus ten, or longer than the trip to Demaratus itself, but that

28

was okay. I have (literally) all the time in the universe.

We transposed to normal space and it was nice to see the stars again. It had been a long time.

Wanderer had a chat with the thedomin in charge of Docking Administration and exchanged his registry code. It was legit enough even if the DA thedomin checked it with Imperial Central Space Vehicle Registry; which, of course, it would. Three centuries back I had set up a dummy Foundation of the self-perpetuating type and *Wanderer* was registered through the Foundation as Foundation property. His registry was renewed automatically every decade.

When the Demaratus DA thedomin compared notes with the Meridian ICSVR thedomin naught would be amiss, although the two ultracomputers might wonder a bit that *Wanderer* had seemingly not touched down on a known planetary body in the past one hundred years or more. But, then, that was the foundation's business and nothing for a couple of nosy thedomins to poke into.

So the Docking Administration took our registry number, issued us a docking permit number and parking plan and we dropped anchor at Demaratus Station. This is one of those monster orbital complexes they were building a few centuries back for planets unfortunate enough to lack a natural moon of their own.

With the ship docked and on emergency self-control I packed my knap and took the scooter over to the nearest terminal entrance. On the way I got a gorgeous view of Demaratus below bathed in sunlight. The terminator was way back at the further limb and the planet made a beautiful spectacle.

Beta Cygni is a binary star in the Cygnus part of the Carina-Cygnus Arm. Beta Cygni A is a yellow star of the Sol type, if a little smaller, and the second

29

component of the planet's primary is a Main Sequence star faintly blue. The binary's system supports six planets of which Demaratus is number four. The mixture of blue and yellow sunlight comes out a light, bright green which must be a little difficult to live with, although I suppose you get used to it in time.

I moored in a vacant scooter bay just inside the entrance, unsuited and took the slidewalk into the terminal proper. Since Demaratus lacks a moon I suppose she doesn't have any tides, although she does have seas and whopping big ones from the spectacular view I had enjoyed on the way over. It must be odd, not having tides.

The terminal was big, crowded, noisy and confusing. It was built in tiers around a central rotunda—each tier stepped back a bit from the tier beneath. I had parked my scooter at an entrance bay on the equator-line which meant I came out into the terminal proper on a tier just half-way up the stack.

The upper levels seemed to be all shops and services. I say a men's wear shop and toyed with the idea of purchasing a suit—for camouflage purposes more than anything else. I was wearing gray one-piece coveralls, the sort of thing we wear under an airsuit. Spacemen call it an "airsuit liner" because it is made to fit under an airsuit and is padded and reinforced at the friction points. But I saw that lots of people in the crowd wore the same kind of coveralls so I decided my clothes would not attract undue attention.

Next to the men's wear shop was one for women. I took a look at the animated display screen and saw that women's fashions were still a weird little world all their own. The dancing, smiling, laughing, cavorting models in the display were clothed (if that's the word) in bewildering things—all sparkly metal tis-

30

sue and gauzy synthetics with lots of bare flesh in between. I admired the scenery profoundly.

And then I felt the mindtouch—

And then it was gone. A fleeting surface probe gone before I could resonate with it and ride the carrier wave back to the telepath who had tried to read me.

I pride myself on my self-control. By not a flicker of involuntary surprise did I show that I was aware of the mental probe. I turned away from the bright colors and graceful moving forms and started down towards the rotunda. There were plenty of people in the vicinity who could have been my telepath but I didn't notice anyone who seemed to show any particular interest in me or my actions.

Well, whoever had tried to probe me, hadn't. I wear a good mindlock when I am out on the town—the best commercial model money can buy. Not that I needed a mindlock for my own protection, you understand. I'm a Star class telepath myself and my own natural shield is far stronger than any commercial job. But why should I give away for free to the first guy who comes along the fact that I happen to be a telepath? Under a commercial mindlock a real telepath can hide perfectly. But my Star class sensitivity is such that even under the over-lapping, heterodyning field of the mindlock I can feel a probe.

And, incidentally, I'm not trying to brag about being a Star. I know we are damn rare and that not one in twenty billion hominids is even born with the telepathic AG24 gene alone, much less with the cerebral fibulation it takes to make Star. No, the fact of the matter is that most immortals eventually develop T-powers if they live long enough. I wasn't born with T, I grew it. I have a theory about this. Take the

31

human mind in infancy: it's inchoate, fumbling and uncoordinated. As a human matures, the mind gradually learns to use its facilities. In a certain sense, you can interpret the growing-up process as one of training the mind until by middle-age you have a sensitive, selective, well-organized instrument up there behind your forehead.

I'm not talking about things like maturity of judgment or taste or anything like that. I mean the process of a mind learning how to *use* its abilities. A child learns to sit, to stand, to walk, run, talk, sing, read and whatever. The body already has all the walk-run-sit muscles and the nerve-endings are, at birth, all plugged into the brain and ready to go. But, in infancy, the brain doesn't know which button to push. Learning to walk is learning to use that part of the brain correctly.

By maturity the brain has learned how to use many of its parts (not all, by a long shot, but enough). But then what happens? The body begins to come apart at its seams; the machine begins to run down. This is the process we call "growing old." The muscles get feeble and flabby, the flesh loses tone and sags, the eyes go weak and the mind grows forgetful and senile. The physiochemical aging process comes along just in time to keep the mind from any further stages of development.

This did not happen to me. I never physically aged past about 34 or 35. My mind continued developing greater flexibility, greater sensitivity, greater body control and better memory. And, eventually, but rather late in the game, it became telepathic; ending up as Star class—the only known Star class mind in hominid history, in point of fact.

But you see now why I can't take any particular pride in being a Star. Being an immortal, I *had* to develop T-powers up in the Star range because that's one of the natural results of immortality. Or that's my theory, anyway. Unfortunately, I can't check my experience against any one else's. Because, as far as I know, I am the only immortal the human race has ever produced.

THREE

But back to business . . . while I was wondering about who had tried to probe me there in front of the dress shop and why, I reached the first tier and stepped over to the rail to look down at the crowds. It could have been a cop. A *proctor* we call them now; but call him by whatever term you will, a cop is still a cop.

Now, there are whole telepathic races, like the Boygyar of Tau Ceti I, the Ptemerae, the Vanalians, and so on. They all developed T-powers in lieu of speech. The Boygyar are non-breathers so, of course, they could not develop the fine art of conversation on anything but a mental level. And the Ptemerae, being insectoid, lack the equipment: voice-box, tongue, lips—the whole works, up to and including lungs. Some of these, like Vanalians, go in for proctoring. Others, like the Boygyar, can't be cops for certain philosophical and humanitarian reasons.

Most of those rare hominids born with the AG24 gene end up working as cops. But a human telepath is so very *rara* an *avis* that there is a hefty premium on his services—too hefty for the small-time locals, which means there are damn few hominid telepaths in the employ of any given planet's proctor service. Most of them end up in government intelligence or working as Citadel agents, which implied my snooper was no local cop but somebody from Imperial intelligence.

Maybe. But if so, what was he doing indiscriminantly probing an innocent guy ogling the pretty models in front of a Demaratus Station dress shop?

35

It didn't make sense. Then.

Down in the rotunda I saw all sorts of people, lots of them with sort of pale, colorless complexions. I assumed (correctly) that these were native Demaratans, as the greenish sunslight would most likely produce that washed-out skin color. But there were also a few bronzed Sirians or maybe Centaurians, a few yellow fellows from the Draconians, an Ildh from Beta Lyrae II in his powered bubble-skimmer and even a tall, swarthy, hawk-faced native Rilké chieftain from far-off Hercules in his suede cloak and *tegraan*-feather galliche. Then the crowd parted to make way for a ponderous, lumbering boyg who peered about with fierce bright humorous orange eyes—small in his vast beaked head.

Such is the power of coincidence! I had just, moments before, been thinking about the Boygyar of Tau Ceti and, lo and behold, here came one dragging by his mighty forty-foot length right under me.

I leaned over the rail and grinned down at the old fella. The Boygyar are just about the nicest thing that ever happened to mankind. We have always been lonely animals. Back in the beginning of things—long before Armstrong took that giant step from the bottom rung of the *Eagle*'s ladder to the rock-strewn surface of Mare Tranquilitas—we had to learn to live with the fact that we shared our planet with a bunch of dumb animals. Not counting the dolphins and the so-called social insects, there was nothing else around that was anywhere near being our intellectual equal. We had to learn to live with loneliness and to get along with just dogs for companionship.

Even after men took that historic step and opened the door to the—*Universe, vast universe, billion-starred and wide*—we still found ourselves alone. The philosophical crystalloids Berengey found on Gany-

36

mede were intelligent enough as far as anyone could tell but we couldn't communicate with them. There were some enigmatic artifacts scattered around the Asteriod Zone but the "lost planet," Sol V, blew up about the time Earth was passing through its Miocene. As for the rest, there was just naked rock, gas giants and chilly lumps of ammonia and methane ice. We had to wait until we got out to the stars to find a friend.

It was an odd fluke that took us to the Tau Ceti system to discover the Boygyar before we got to Epsilon Eridani where we met the Ptemerae. Odd because Tau Ceti is 10.9 lightyears from Sol and Epsilon Eridani only 10.8 and, although one-tenth of a lightyear doesn't mean much of anything these days, it meant a hell of a lot back then. I shudder to think what might have been the results if we had made contact with the Ptemerae *first*. They are just about the most uncooperative, vile-tempered, xenophobic, inhospitable and self-centered bunch of bugs in known space. Why, one look at them and we might have packed up our hardware and gone back home—to stay! But the Boygyar were something else.

The human race and the Boygyar have a psycho-emotional empathy, a perfect affinity, for each other that is one of the nicest things that ever happened. To look at the "dragons" of Tau Ceti I, our friendship would seem most unlikely, at least on the surface. We are so very different in so many ways. Remember Choy y'th-Thoh's famous definition of Man in the *Ninth Chronicle?*—"a warm-blooded, oxygen-breathing, bisexual, erect, mammalian, bipedal war-maker"?

Well, by those criteria, you could define a Boyg as a "frigid-blooded, non-breathing, asexual, non-erect reptilian, sextupedal pacifist" which does not even begin to convey an impression of what they *look* like.

Take a full-grown triceratops, cross him with a super-crocodile, stretch him out to an average forty-foot length from beak-point to tail-tip, plate him over with an extra two-foot-thick layer of the lumpiest, densest, toughest hide this side of poly-tungsten-steel, give him an average lifespan of four thousand years and the most superb telepathic brain known to modern science and you've got yourself a Boyg.

Never mind that he weighs up to sixty tons in his stocking feet—all six of 'em. Never mind that he lives bare in hard vacuum, chews up raw copper ore for lunch and lumbers around in a hide so tough a 50 cm. hand-laser doesn't even give him a tickle. He is Man's best and greatest friend.

A less-likely friendship could hardly have been imagined. We have so little in common. The Boygyar have no wars, no crime, no sense of personal possessiveness; no love, romance, marriage or even a sex-life worth speaking of (unless you consider spore-budding reproduction a sex-life); no art, music, sculpture, drama, poetry, literature or even a language, for that matter. But they have something a lot better. To them, life itself is an artform. Literally, each Boyg tries to make his life a triumphant work of beautiful art.

I wonder how the history of good old *terra firma* would have read, if Man had come up with that idea? Every man his own Marcus Aurelius—his own Socrates—his own Christ? I wonder?

Unlikely as hell, but get along we did from the very beginning. We had a natural affinity of some rare kind and we both felt it from the first. It was the two broken halves of something coming together and making a whole, when Man and Boyg first met there on that airless chunk of naked rock under the eye-searing glare of Tau Ceti.

So I leaned on the rail and smiled down fondly on the Boyg as the immense parareptilian waddled his slow, bowlegged way through the rotunda. He looked huge and monstrous and fearsome enough to be something from a puffhead's nightmare dreamed-up after an all day puffweed orgy. But there were about fifteen kids climbing all over him squealing with delight. Including one tow-headed toddler gleefully nestled down between the backridge of his neck-carapace and his twin horns. Unknowingly, the blond tyke was drumming his (or her) heels right in those wise, kindly, twinkling, humorous orange eyes under the huge horny browridges—which was okay, a little heel-drumming was not about to cause the old duffer any discomfort. A Boyg can take a 34-magnum lead slug on the "naked" eyeball without even making him blink.

Then the great Boyg slowed to a shuffling stop, craned his five-ton head and peered up directly at me.

This person says you have an unfriend here, Saul Everest, the Boyg telepathed.

FOUR

Well, I never yet saw a commercial mindlock that could even slow down a Boygyar telepathic communication much less stop one cold, so I wasn't particularly surprised. Neither was there any mystery in the fact that the Boyg knew my name—one of my names, anyway. With an average lifespan forty centuries long, the parareptilians of Tau Ceti I are the only sentient race in known space that live anything remotely comparable to my own lifespan, whose length I could hardly be expected to know, since it isn't over yet. In other words, it was not unlikely that I had known this particular Boyg a ways back. But I knew I had never met him because I would have recognized the characteristic waveform of his communication, which among telepathic races is as distinctive, if not more so, than the variance between one human voice and another.

No, the Boyg simply read my current name among the superficial stuff on the surface level of my mind. I did the same now to his mind; I resonated with the heterodyning shield of my mindlock (not wanting to turn it off with an enemy in snooping range) and beamed a reply back to him.

Thank you for the information, Doctor Einstein, I replied.

The Boygyar, being non-breathers, have no vocal apparatus. It would be quite superfluous on airless Tau Ceti I. Thus, having no spoken language and remembering what I just said about the individual characteristics of telepathic waves, you can see why

41

they never invented the concept of individual names. (Their race name, Boygyar, was coined by the Scandinavian spaceship commander who first encountered them. Something in their ponderous, good-humored and friendly monstrousness reminded him inescapably of "the Great Boyg" in Ibsen's *Peer Gynt*. The name caught on, and stuck.)

But when the terrestrial crews of the *Lucian of Samosata* and the *Robert A. Heinlein* first made planet-fall on Tau Ceti I, they found enormous difficulties in telling one Boyg from another. One seventy-ton, forty-foot dragon looks remarkably like all the rest, you see. The Boygyar—who rapidly became great students of human history—took care of this problem by adopting names which they borrowed from the various figures they most admired in our history.

Not that this did not eventually produce problems of its own! I have known eleven Boygyar in my time named Francoise Marie Arouet de Voltaire, to say nothing of nine Dr. Martin Luther King, Jr.'s, and any number of Socrateses. There was even one Boygyar colleague of mine in Citadel who went by the name of Ptah-hotep. Obviously he found himself in sympathy with the shrewd, practical, yet humanistic doctrines of the Egyptian philosopher of remotest antiquity.

I was wondering about that, I went on. *I felt the mindtouch, even through my shielding. Maybe you can point him out to me, sir?*

Alas, no. By the egg of my first ancestor, I was not really paying attention, to my great shame. Will you accept the apologies of this worthless and inattentive person? he returned, dolefully.

I gently informed him that it was okay and that I was in his debt for the information that my snooper *was* an "unfriend" of mine. Our simian traits of anger and combativeness are quite alien and incomprehensible to the peaceful and philosophical parareptilians, and "unfriend" is about as close as they can come to our word *enemy*. Incidentally, I call Doctor Einstein "he" despite the fact that a Boyg is about as sexless as a tree. The simile is quite apt (and not original with me), since the dragons of Tau Ceti reproduce by a process of spore-budding not unlike certain trees. Boygyar in the embryonic phase are enclosed in a tough, membranous casing, so the use of the word "egg" in Doctor Einstein's phrase is not a mis-translation.

But even a technically sexless sentient being tends in his fundamental temperament and personality towards one polarity or the other and although I have known a few "motherly" Boygyar in my time, and even a couple of fussy, comfortable "aunties," most Boygyar come across as essentially male. Certainly Doctor Einstein had an unmistakably masculine timbre and lean sinewy style to him.

I asked him if he had overheard any plans concerning me but he had perceived only a sensation of overt hostility in the questing probe. And, although he had not "tuned in" to the probe in time to trace it to its source, he had received a vague impression of, and he mentally shaped, a waveform in three dimensions. I couldn't make much out of it. It could have been anybody's. But I thanked him for his time and trouble and watched him go lumbering off across the rotunda to his craft.

So my snooper was definitely after *me* and not just making random probes of everybody in the terminal. In a rather disquieting way, that was nice to know. It is good to be sure about such things.

I came down to the rotunda, got a temporary Demaratan credit card, bought a ticket for the shuttle to Demaratus proper and went through customs. I had no fear that any of the hardware I was wearing would be spotted on the search screens since most of it is ceramic or plastic and of the same density as organic materials. That which isn't is disguised as the normal run of masculine jewelry—two rings, a personal phone, a pocket terory, a solid (seemingly solid, that is) iridium criode, a timer, miscellaneous hard change and a pack of cigarettes.

I went up to the booth and gave the proctor my Citizen's card. It was a fake, of course, but a good one. It would pass personal scrutiny but not a verifier test, as I had no way of impregnating the thin wafer of synthetic crystal with radio-coded molecules. However, just before the proctor slid it in the slot of the verifier, I sent a probe down through his surface layers and depressed the consciousness center of his mind. He went "to sleep" for about five seconds and while in that state he "dreamed" that he had put my card in the verifier and received a clean reading. No one else in line noticed that all he did was put the card in the slot and put his finger on the stud—without pressing down to activate it. It was over in no time. He handed the card back to me and glanced at the iron holstered on my hip.

"You have a permit for that weapon, Cn. Everest?"

"Certainly, officer," I smiled, handing him another card. This one was blank but my probe was still inserted in his consciousness center and he thought he saw the regular permit registry. He handed it back without comment. Then I joined the line waiting for the next shuttle and in fifteen minutes I was on my way down to the planet.

My fellow-passengers were the usual cross-section of humanity you would expect: a couple of families with kids on their way back home after a vacation

44

off-planet; a few Naval officers in regulation dress blacks; several business executive types with knaps full of important papers, including one pudgy, balding specimen making a big production out of his lapfull of contracts and dictating urgent memoranda into the whisper-mike of his wrist recorder. There was even an Imperial courier in the Tregephontane colors carrying a cassette locked to his wrist, its self-destruct seal prominently displayed. And a number of Station personnel on their way down for any number of reasons.

I probed them all, curious to see if my "unfriend," as Doctor Einstein called him, was among my fellow-travelers. If he was, he wore a good mindlock, as I might have expected.

Come to think of it, there was a rather large percentage of my fellow-passengers in the shuttle who wore mindlocks. There was nothing really suspicious about this, but it was an interesting datum.

The courier wore one which was regulation. So did most of the senior Naval officers which was normal. And the business types, too, including the show-off with the lap full of important papers and the wrist recorder.

I probed everybody not wearing mind-protection and found no one who was particularly interested in a tall, black-haired guy with a heavy space-tan and grey eyes to match his airsuit-liner coveralls— except one waitress with eyes tattooed in metallic inks, planet-bound for the weekend, who thought I was pretty cute.

Then there was the girl. I wondered why she was wearing a mindlock. She looked about twenty and she looked spectacular. She wore one of those three-piece, skimpy, sparkling metal-tissue jobs I had been admiring in the dress shop display with plenty of bronze flesh showing. Particularly a sensational pair of legs bare to the upper thigh. Her coiffure was one of those incredible plasticined constructions—lacy, sculpted, filled with little witch-lights. Her pupils had been tattooed a fashionable ruby red and her face was done in glow paint. But under all the cosmetics, it was a good face with a small, stubborn jaw, a pert little nose and a wide, soft, watermelon-pink mouth.

I wondered why she was wearing a mindlock. She certainly didn't look like the executive type. But you never can tell. She might have been somebody's private secretary. If so, he must have been a Very Important somebody for his gal friday to go around in a 200-unit Executron mindlock. But then, in these days when everybody has an office model thedomin, only the Very Important and Very Wealthy top hierarchy execs could afford the anachronistic luxury of a private, human-type secretary, so it figured. Industrial espionage is big these days and she could have a cortex full of her boss' big pending deals.

Naturally, I didn't try to probe anyone wearing a mindlock. If my unfriend *was* aboard, he was a telepath and might feel my probe. But I took a good look at everybody and I would remember their faces in case I ran into them again. An eidetic memory is another thing an immortal develops. And mine had saved my life many times.

FIVE

We landed without incident at Dorion City, hub of the planetary transportation web. I mingled with the crowd and eventually found my way to the taxi area. I picked one—out of the middle of the row, still being cautious—and directed it to take me to a city on the interior of the continent, a place called Dekalb, where the astronomical association had its headquarters. Then I settled back, smoked an aromatique and listened to a newscast.

All of this would have been much simpler if I could have landed at Dekalb in *Wanderer* and gone about my business. But orbit-to-surface landings are frowned upon by the proctors of most heavily-urban planets. You need a damn good reason and there are several yards of good old-fashioned red tape involved and such a landing would have attracted an awful lot of attention. And the one thing I wanted most to avoid was attracting attention. What could be more innocent and innocuous than parking at Demaratus Station and coming down with a shuttle-full of tourists?

I kept an eye on one of my two rings. The band and setting were made of pallium and the stone, as any jeweler would have sworn to, was a nice ordinary Bergeron IV sundrop. Since the gem was not fluorescing, was, in fact, quiescent, I knew nobody had planted a tell-tale in or on the cab. And from the lack of any activity from the thing in my left bootheel, it seemed nobody had a searchbeam fix on the cab, either. So far, so good. It began to look as if I could relax.

I leaned back and watched a local *psi*-ball championship game on the newscast.

I had never visited this particular planet before, for all my millennia; there must be upwards of half a million inhabited planets in the galaxy by now and even the Eternal can't visit all that real estate—not that I didn't do quite a bit of zapping around in my livelier days. But Demaratus—although an urban center, home of a galactically-famous college and once the residence of the Archpoet himself, not to mention its place in scientific history—is not so important a world. In fact (I was lazily thinking during the cab's flight) it looked like a sleepy little backwater.

This particular cab was an older model than some I could have picked. Old and creaky. It took a good forty-five minutes, Local reckoning, to get me from the center of Dorion City into the stacking pattern over Dekalb. That was almost as much time as it had taken *Wanderer* to get here from Home! But the game on the newscast kept me from expiring from sheer boredom and the scenery was gorgeous. It had been a long time since I had rested my eyes on grassy plains and virgin mountains and meandering rivers and I enjoyed the trip.

Once over Dekalb, I gave the local street address of the Association and it took another five minutes to reach the building which was set out in the country surrounded by parks and gardens.

I paid the tab with the credit card issued to me at Demaratus Station and got out in the parking lot. My sensories were out searching the vicinity for any suspicious activity. While the cab was flying me cross-country, *Wanderer* had informed me via the tiny mini-phone surgically implanted in the mastoid bone behind my right ear that a private gig had been snooping around his parking area. He had detected a searchbeam and subelectronic probes of three different types.

This sounded like trouble. Of course, *Wanderer* carried every kind of protective screen you would expect from a heavy Arion-class dreadnaught which meant it could take on anything up to and including fleet action without even cracking a shield. But that was in itself suspicious since my ship was seemingly just a private yacht. It implied my cover *had* been blown and that the Opposition (whoever they were) were on to me. Well, I would just have to let things sort themselves out as best they would. I was here to get some information and that came first.

I went in the main entrance and flashed another one of my collection of cards at the receptionist, who was a thedomin. This card, which was legit, identified me as an Imperial courier, Herald class, on direct orders from His Magnificence, himself. This got fast action as you might expect. A Herald-class courier is personally appointed by a regnant Imperator as a member of his personal Suite. He is answerable to no one but the Imperator and when on Imperial business, he is above the reach of any and all local laws, regulations and ordinances. A Herald can thus go anywhere he pleases, at any time, without impediment. The Imperator has about two hundred such aides and who they are or where they go is, literally, nobody's business.

The card, I repeat, was legit. As a matter of fact, a Herald's brassard (as it is more correctly called) is incapable of being counterfeited. It is a sigil of organic crystal whose molecular structure is keyed to the individual alpha-profile of the Herald's own brain. Its inscription is luminous and legible only when on the person of the Herald to whose brainwaves it is keyed. In the hands of another, the brassard is blank and opaque.

Mine was legit and functional because I issued it to myself a good thousand years back during one of my occasional appearances on the Imperial stage as Prince Regent during the minority of Uxorian the Great after Citadel deposed his older brother, the late and unlamented Arion IV, who founded the House of Arthenis.

Anyway, I got the files I wanted and a private booth and projector. I unlimbered my knap, took out and set up a beam-proof privacy screen and started looking at the pretty pictures.

I had asked for a set of visual sightings taken along the Rim during the six-month interval my private R-2 monitor had recorded major fluctuations in the galaxy's magnetic field. Now I fixed them on the projector's screen and took out the key magnetigraphs received from R-2 and duplicated by my house thedomin on overlay transparencies. I lined up the coordinates of the two sets of transparencies and locked them into place.

The visual studies of the Rim were reversed to black-on-white for greater definition of detail. The magnetigrams were an undulating series of red lines, each labelled according to its intensity with a green circle marking the approximate center of the disturbance. By coordinating the two sets of transparencies, I should be able to get visual confirmation of the presence of the Intruder.

I got exactly nothing.

The areas covered by the green circles just showed blank space on the Association's photograms.

I tagged the center-of-disturbance areas on the photograms, took off the overlays and pushed the magnification up to max. Still nothing. Nothing at all.

I was sweating. Literally. It was hot in that damn little booth and a privacy field even inhibits the movements of air molecules which means I wasn't getting the benefit of the office air conditioning. Or was I sweating for another reason?

One last check. I used the booth phone and called the files thedomin for further confirmation. Of course, modern astronomers don't depend on visible-light photograms alone. When they scrutinize an area of space, they do so all up and down the spectrum. There are some stars that don't radiate at all in the 4000-to-7700 Angstrom octave of visible light but really belt it out up in the 100 km to 1 mm Hertzian wavelengths. And still other stars invisible in the light and radio octaves that radiate like crazy in the wavelengths of cosmic rays or even up in the trans-cosmics. In fact, there are no less than twenty-seven known stars that radiate entirely in the 10^{25} cycles-per-second frequency of Cherensky radiation.

So naturally modern astronomers use the whole electromagnetic spectrum and a battery of gadgets up to and including asdar. What I wanted to see was a composite transparency covering all 67+ octaves of the spectrum. The Association files thedomin was fully capable of making such composites and in about ten minutes Local I had them in my sweaty little hands.

Nothing.

Absolutely nothing. I checked and double-checked but no object of stellar or even planetary mass had occupied the center of disturbance during the sighting times.

Just what did this mean?

Well, for one thing, it did *not* mean there was nothing there. It just meant there was nothing there that was radiating in any octave up or down the elec-

51

tromagnetic spectrum, *i.e.*, the mystery object I had labeled "the Intruder" was not a star, rogue or otherwise. Unless . . .

Unless it was a *dark* star. The dead, cold, burnt-out cosmic clinker of what had once been a blazing stellar fireball. Now, this was not impossible. Dark stars were known although they are about as rare as scales on a Pterian. They are probably a lot less rare than they seem to be. After all, how do you detect something in the pitch-black night of space if it is not radiating energy? There are only two ways: you run into it, or you detect it on your asdar scope. And, unfortunately, the Rim Star Astronomical Association had never had any particular reason to search that moving area of space with asdar.

Neither had they thought to use the mu/meson detector which would have to report the presence of a mobile planet—*if* the Magellanics, or whoever was behind this Intruder phenomenon, used our kind of propulsive system.

If it hadn't been for my study of fluctuations in the galaxy's magnetic field, we might never have known the Intruder was there at all. That is, until it was ready to begin doing whatever it had travelled here to do . . .

When I returned the transparencies to the Association's files, I invoked Herald's Seal on the whole thing. Under the Seal, top secrecy is imposed and the penalties for release of Sealed information are dire indeed. The Association's Director, a dry-voiced Centaurian, in my presence, instructed the files thedomin to "forget" which files had been requested by me and in fact, to "forget" that I had ever been to the Association headquarters at all. That went for the office thedomin, too, in its facet as front-desk receptionist.

My business with the Association now finished, I

became aware of a yawning void within. I glanced at my timer. It was then exactly 15:24 Standard. I had lifted ship from Home almost exactly five Standard hours ago, so no wonder I wanted some lunch. Since the Association building was way out in the suburbs, I presumed the building included cafeteria facilities for the staff. I asked the Director about this and he instructed an aide to escort me to the automat insisting I be the guest of the Association. He declined to join me as it was 14:00 Local time, the middle of the afternoon, and he and his employees had long since lunched.

So I had the cafeteria all to myself which was okay with me. Besides eating, I had a little hard thinking to do. The autochef whipped up a Narlionid seaflower salad for me, smoking-hot sliced iophodon steak from Barnassa in succulent spice-gravy and a pot of fragrant stimulac. It was a good lunch, all but the stimulac. There's just no substitute for genuine coffee from Brazil, Terra and no conceivable variety of caffeine-derivative can ever capture its aroma. But until I was back on Home, I was stuck with stimulac and had to like it.

But I wasn't really thinking of my gut. I was thinking about the Intruder. Who he was, where he was from and why he was here. Was he, in fact, a snooper manned or sent here by some Magellanic sentience? Or was he just the burnt-out ash-heap of what had once been a star wandering rogue and lifeless? Even a burnt-out dead coal of a star has stellar mass enough to cause major disturbances in the magnetic field of a galaxy. But so too would a manned and mobile planet sent here from Beyond on a mission of surveillance.

It was a pretty problem. And I was not putting my money on the Intruder turning out to be anything so innocent as the dead husk of a burnt-out star. And what in the Plenum did all this have to do with whoever tried to read me back on Demaratus Station and the members of the still-unidentified Opposition who had sent out a gig to probe the defenses of *Wanderer*.

What possible connection could there be between a mysterious magnetic disturbance way out in the Range Stars at the very end of the second arm of this galactic spiral and a gang of crooks, including at least one criminal telepath, hanging around Demaratus Station?

It didn't seem to make much sense.

Well. Obviously, I wasn't going to find the answers to any of these questions here. It looked like my next move was going to be a long trip out to the Range Stars where I was overdue for a little "Intruder-hunting." The Director had picked up the tab for my lunch—they obviously don't have a visit from one of Kermian XIX's Herald-class couriers every day in the week—so I headed for the front door.

I got as far as the landing flat before I felt the tangle-field close about my limbs. I looked up to see my old friend the pudgy businessman—he of the lapful of contracts and the wrist recorder. He wasn't using the recorder now. Both fat little hands were full of a lot of stungun. And the muzzle was aimed straight at the center of my forehead.

I got one quick look at his cold, cunning little pig-eyes and the gloating, self-satisfied smile on his thick lips and I knew I had found my snooper. Or, rather, he had found me.

Then the gun went off and I went to sleep for a while.

SIX

The mind has many layers, and its defenses are flexible and ingenious.

Have you ever been on the receiving end of a stungun? Back in the old days we called it, or its great-grandpappy, a neuronic scrambler. A stungun wave is tuned to the same generic wavelength as human thought. Actually, it's beautiful in its simplicity. It does nothing more than "jam" the neurons. Overloaded, they "burn out," temporarily of course. This would cause intolerable pain to the consciousness center so it just goes to sleep for a while until normal service is resumed and the mental switchboard is functional again.

See what I mean? How beautifully simple. The neuronic connections can handle a temporary overload in time and the brain does not receive any permanent damage—not from just one stungun bolt, anyway. I have known murders to be committed with the weapon, for it will kill if used on the brain long enough. But anybody can take one bolt and wake up a half an hour later with nothing worse than a slight headache.

How much neater than the old caveman trick of bashing somebody in the back of the head with a hard, heavy object! That kind of treatment can result in all kinds of unpleasant end-products up to and including brain concussions and cracked skulls. And if all you want to do is put someone out of commission for a brief interval of time, a stungun is the tool for you.

But there is a part of the brain that never sleeps. Deep in the unconscious mind level is a subsidiary consciousness center which handles the involuntary physical activities like heartbeat, breathing and so on. And the T-power centers are located in the unconscious mind. Thus, when the bolt from the fat man's stungun knocked out my conscious controls, I did not entirely go to sleep.

For the brain has weird and wondrous ways of protecting itself. My subsidiary consciousness knew I was in danger and under attack. And almost in the same microsecond that his fat fingers squeezed the trigger and blew my mind I launched a probe into his brain. He wore a mindlock but adrenalin was pumping through my system and my T-centers were blasting through that lock with every erg of power I could command. Even as I blacked out completely I was through his shield and inserted deep into his sensories.

I opened his eyes and tried to look at myself. The shock of his shield breaking down had stunned and shaken him and this was fortunate for me, as it took just about all I had to get through that shield.

I pulled his eyes into focus and watched my limp body sag groundwards through the tangle-field like something photographed in slow motion. It was a weird, uncanny feeling. Of all the many times I had seized control of another mind, I had never experienced so strongly this sensation which I can only label, very inadequately, a feeling of "dissociation." The term is inexact but I can think of no better way to describe it. I was not in the least aware of my own body; it was numb and dead and not the slightest trace or tinge of physical sensation carried over into my mental condition. I felt emotionless, disembodied and ghostly. It was as if I had died and had at the very moment of death managed to project myself into the body of another.

I was in a very dangerous predicament. With only one probe inserted into his brain I had a very inadequate control over him. Usually, when I take over another man's brain, I like to sink six or eight probes into the various brain centers. This time I barely had my foot in the door, so to speak. My control was only partial. I soon discovered I had to move my probe from center to center and could only control him one action at a time.

A shadow fell over the sunlit scene. I craned his head and made him look up stiffly. About twenty feet above a large black limousine hovered, descending slowly. It came to rest a few yards away. Doors slid aside and two hard-faced men got out.

"What's the matter, Dom? We waited for you to signal us down, but nothing happened," one of them said quickly. He stepped over to the edge of the tangle-field and grinned at my body. "That's him, eh?" he chuckled.

My fat businessman, Dom, must have looked odd under my crippled control—pale, strained and half-awake—because the other thug examined Dom puzzledly and said: "You all right, or did he blast you, or what?"

I struggled for control of the vocal apparatus.

"I'm—okay," I made him say. My control was inadept and clumsy. I couldn't modulate the speech center well enough to put any inflection or tone in his voice. The words came out in a harsh croak.

"Well . . . what are we waiting for?" the second man said roughly. "Let's pack him in the car and hit the sky before some flackin' office type comes along and sees the whole show!"

"Right," I muttered. "Turn off the—tangler."

He gave me a baffled glare.

‹ "You sure he didn't beam you or something?" he snarled angrily. "You got the damn powerpack in your japon."

I grunted something through Dom's numb lips and fumbled the gun into my other hand while I forced one hand into the japon pocket. My half-paralyzed fingers rubbed smooth metal, found a catch and closed it. Dust, held aloft in the gluey suspension of the field, swirled free as the current cut off.

The driver stuck his head out of the black limousine and called nervously:

"Hey, step it up you guys! Somebody's liable to come along any minute."

Suddenly my control slipped. Dom was recovering from his dazed condition. I lost hold on his vocal apparatus and he uttered a strangled gasp. The second man turned to snarl something at me. I pointed one of Dom's hands, the one still clinging to the gun, and on sudden impulse managed to cry out "*P-p-proctors!*"

The two men spun about with startled oaths to peer in the direction I was pointing the arm. I didn't dare waste time. My control over this body was rapidly deteriorating. I closed one finger over the trigger and shot them down with the stungun. I had no time to aim at the back of their heads. I just held the gun out stiffly and jerked my arm back and forth like someone spraying a lawn.

They fell suddenly, sprawling awkwardly like jointed puppets whose strings have been cut all at once.

"Hey, what the kaking hell, you lousy son of a—!" the driver screeched as I gunned down his two friends.

I jerked the body around, staggering and almost falling. Dom was awake and fighting me now half

58

crazy with terror. The sensation of sharing your mind with an intruder is a particularly horrible one. He was very strong and I was near the end of my strength. But, oddly enough, his own terror hurt him and helped me. Instead of digging in tenaciously and fighting every inch of the way, he was striking and flailing in every direction, as it were, wasting his strength. I dug deep into his main control center, thus gaining a "shadow" control of several motor centers at once, dragged him around bodily and sprayed stungun fire all over the front of the car.

I got the driver just as his hand was digging viciously into his pocket for a weapon. His mouth was spewing curses. Then he gagged and went silent, mouth sagging wet and loose, eyes rolling glassily, as my bolt took him right between the eyes. He slumped across the controls like a dead thing.

Now I was fighting for my very life.

This fat, fussy little man may have looked foolish and ineffectual but he fought like a roaring madman. I clung to consciousness sinking my slender probe deeper and deeper into his mind. Three times he almost tore me loose. Three times I managed to retain my tenuous grip on his brain but each time my grip was weaker. I felt like a dead leaf being whipped and battered in a howling windstorm. The next shouting gust would doubtless tear me loose, to whirl away and be lost amid the darkness of the inchoate storm.

Suddenly, as dazed and half-blinded I clung to awareness with slipping, weakening fingers, I became conscious that I had sunk my probe so deeply into his mind that I was anchored in the subconscious levels, only a hair's-breadth from the involuntary muscular controls. With one last desperate surge of fainting strength, I locked my grip around the nearest center and paralyzed it—

59

—And stopped his lungs!

He gagged—gasped—face crimsoning, eyes bulging with pain and terror, as he discovered he could no longer pump air into his oxygen-starved lungs.

Then his vision blackened and he crumpled on the ground, heels kicking, open palms drumming frantically for air.

Just as his consciousness flickered and went out, I tore my probe out and drove it deep in the motor centers again. I dragged his limp body to its feet, sent it reeling and tottering over to where my own body sprawled unconscious, bent down clumsily and grabbed the front of my suit, and sent the fat man stumbling towards the open door of the limousine dragging the dead weight of my own body behind him.

It took a thousand years. Every staggering step took an infinity of effort. I had to concentrate every atom of my exhausted powers to keep Dom on his feet. My limp body seemed to weigh a megtaton. It was like trying to drag a dead swamp dragon through an Algolian marsh with one hand. Dom's eyes were half-closed and unfocused and I honestly could not afford the effort to clear his vision. But my withdrawal from his unconscious mind had relaxed my paralyzing grip on his involuntary muscular centers and he was breathing again, drawing in great heavy gulps of air into his screaming lungs, his pounding heart driving red tides of strength into his half-dead body.

At the end of a thousand years I reached the car and half leaned against it. My entire being was permeated with the urgent need to get away fast before one of the men I had stungunned revived. Perhaps I had only grazed one and he would recover before

I did. Perhaps another car was hovering to land with reinforcements. *I—had to—get away—*

With a surge of strength, I dragged my lifeless body up and through the rear door. It sprawled across the seat like a rag doll. Then I lurched forward and jammed Dom into the front seat. I was clinging to consciousness now by a slender thread. Roaring tides of darkness rose all about me, ready to engulf me, to drag me down and drown me in a vortex of thunder. I sent Dom's hand thrusting out blindly for the door control—found it, by some miracle—thrust it home and felt the front and rear doors *snikk* into place.

He was reviving again and I was weaker than ever before, at the utmost limits of my strength. I splayed his fingers and stabbed blindly at the control studs. They say the controls are so simple nowadays that any imbecile can drive a car. I hoped that was so. Somehow I made the car ascend to cruising level, locked it on the autocontrol beam for Dorion City and fell back against the cushions, locked in a mental battle with Dom.

I had to put him out of operation and quick. I could feel myself letting go, sliding down into darkness. I reached out and grabbed the gun from the driver who still lay crumpled over the controls. I twisted my hand around until the muzzle stared its cold steel eye at the fat man's face.

Inside his mind he was screaming something but I was too tired to listen. I pulled the trigger and let go of his mind, recoiling my probe at last.

The poor fat man. I hadn't realized; I hadn't looked. I guess, with what dazed remnants of my wits I still retained, I blindly assumed the driver was carrying a stungun too.

61

But he wasn't. He was carrying a Barringer .23 mm and it blew the fat man's head off.

My probe was still uncoiling its way out of his mind when it happened. I don't want to dwell on what it feels like for a telepath to be in even *partial* occupation of a living brain when that brain dies . . .

It's not a matter of anything as gross as mere pain. It's not even a question of anything as simple as empathetic shock, or the emotional horror of the experience. Nothing so crude as that.

If you are a telepath, chances are you may have been *en rapport* with another telepath at the moment of his death. The experience is not so uncommon. But few telepaths below my own rare (all right, then, *unique*) level of T-power are strong enough to be able to seize and take control of another mind. Occupancy, even partial, as I say, is different from just being in communication. The psychic impact is horrendous. Indescribable. I don't want to say more than this about the experience. I would rather forget it.

You see, I died once, long ago. Really died. I am not talking about the sort of "technical" death that sometimes happens under delicate surgery. Then the medico shoots a jet of stiminol-17 directly into the heart or uses psychostatic stimulus on the brain cortex and you come back. It's not uncommon and generally the poor gink being operated on never even knows he was technically dead there for a few seconds. But I *died* in *Wanderer II* that time, forty-six centuries ago, when the United Systems went bust and Nordonn set up his military dictatorship. Not only was I dead—*really* dead—but I was dead for four hundred years.

But that's private and personal stuff. Part of my own secret history and my own business. The Pseudodeath was a long time ago and it's better forgotten. Except, how do you ever manage to forget something like . . . having died?

Anyway, that too is another story. It doesn't belong here. Perhaps, unless this venture in autobiography palls on me at length, that story will be told some day. But not here and not now.

But, as you can imagine, I know what it's like to die. Once is bad enough. No one should have to go through it *twice*. For the fat man, at least, there would be no second time. He was splattered all over the interior of the car.

SEVEN

Three hours or so later, a good hot meal under my belt, a tall frosty drink in my hand, relaxing in a soft pneumo, I was beginning to feel almost human again.

My prisoner sat bolt upright in the chair opposite my own. *He* was most uncomfortable. Or so he looked. His long bony face was pale and wet and his loose mouth worked nervously. His eyes prowled restlessly from side to side, searching every corner of the room, as if hunting for hidden foes. His arms and legs dangled limp and useless. I had not bound him. I had not needed artificial constraints. All I had done was cut off his major motor nerves, effecting temporary paralysis.

It was good to sit and rest after the lively afternoon I had enjoyed—if that's the word. I had revived from the effects of the stungun just as the limousine entered the limits of Dorion City and was automatically guided into the stacking pattern. I was one hellova mess. For one thing, Dom was splattered all over me, sticky red goo and greyish gobbets of brain. My face felt raw as if it had been dragged for twenty feet over sharp pebbles—which it had. I was weak as an invalid, shaky as a puffhead in the middle stages of full withdrawal and I had the very Imperator of all headaches.

I could hardly manage to think through the blinding waves of sheer agony that throbbed through my skull. And when I tried to move, to sit up, I felt like the victim of the Haburz torture-cult does at the end of the Seven Holy Days.

I got my knap off and pawed through it for my medikit. An intravenous jet of stiminol cleared my head as if by magic. A local anesthetic took the burn and sting out of my raw face and I treated the abrasions with quick-healing gel and covered them from sight with a cosmetic dye. Three go-pills and I felt back in one piece again, wrapped and insulated in a glowing haze of synthetic euphoria.

Luckily, this was a custom-designed luxury-class limousine and whoever put it together had not gone easy on the units. It had a built-in bar and even a miniscule lavatory. I washed away the blood, brains and grime, and sponged my clothes clean—they were plasticine celoflex so the dirt didn't set in but wiped right off. These tasks done, I tossed back a triple jigger of excellent wineapple brandy and started to think.

I could not stay aloft on automatic forever. Before long a traffic proctor would buzz up alongside to see if I was all right. Of course, the smart thing to do would be to park this heap somewhere and take the shuttle back up to Demaratus Station where *Wanderer* was docked. Once inside my own ship I would be as safe as a man could wish.

But, of course, this was just what I could *not* do. For one thing, I had a corpse in the front seat. And even more importantly, I had a prisoner. The driver was only stungunned; he would be waking up soon and his mind would be a well of valuable information. I had a real live member of the Opposition in hand. It was a priceless chance to find out just what in the Nine Scarlet Hells of Garkhoy this thing was all about.

But I needed a haven—someplace where I would be undisturbed and could dig into the driver's mind at my leisure. Of course, I could just keep the limousine in cruising orbit around Dorion City while I excavated his memory for data but that was a wee bit risky. I still had a very dead fat man on my hands and the first traffic proctor who came along might want to know why one of my passengers was minus a head.

Then it occurred to me that all I had to do was ditch the car someplace. The gun dangled from the corpse's fat fingers. His prints were all over the trigger-guard. It was an open-and-shut case of suicide.

I finally picked the best hiding-place in the galaxy —a first class hotel. The more expensive your room the less the management cares what you do in it. I kept the limousine in the stacking pattern for a time while I searched the pockets of the two men in the front seat. The fat man was carrying a huge wad of units, in local currency, which was perfect. For obvious reasons, I would rather pay for the room in cash than use my temporary Demaratan credit card which is registered in my name and Citizen's Code.

I found nothing in their pockets beyond some money and the usual personal articles. Nothing to identify them or link them with any kind of organization.

I opaqued the windows, picked out the biggest and most expensive hotel in Dorion City, the Imperator Ralric II, and parked the limousine in the basement garage. As I had guessed, it was fully robotic and had no attendants. I found the keys in the driver's pocket, locked the car and went up to the lobby to register. The room clerk took in my rather unprepossessing appearance with incredulous eyes but he turned all smiles and "Yes, Sirs" when I ordered the Imperial Suite and paid for it with a wad of units nearly big enough to fill the luggage I did not have. I got my key, went back to the basement, unloaded

67

the driver just as he was beginning to return to the waking world again, laid him out cold for the second time with a blow from the edge of my hand to the clump of ganglia just behind his ear and carried him up to my floor in the gravity well. I used the freight tube rather than one of the passenger tubes and luckily, we did not encounter anyone on the way up, although I was ready to alter their memory of the incident in case we did run into anyone. I got him into the suite, locked the door, turned on the privacy field I had last used back at the Association headquarters when I checked the astronomical transparencies and tossed the unconscious man in the nearest chair. Then I headed for the facilities. No 'fresher for me, I wanted to wallow in a steaming hot bath until the aches and pains went away for good.

One good long soak, one great half-hour under the tender brutalities of the robot masseuse, one inch thick induction-broiled steak and one superchilled bottle of fifteen-year-old champagne, and I was back in the land of the living again. It was now 20:04— early evening. My guest was awake and yelling himself hoarse inside the soundproof privacy field. I had left instructions with the desk that I was not to be disturbed even if the hotel caught on fire. I went over and stretched out in the pneumochair with a tall drink and smoked, surveying my guest calmly.

He had the pale, washed-out complexion of a native Demaratan, so either the Opposition was based here or, if they were headquartered off-planet, he might be just a local thug hired for a one-time grab. Well, we would soon see.

By now he had worked himself into a prime case of the jitters, which meant he would be a soft probe. That was okay with me. After my exhausting mental tussle with the fat man whose headless cadaver still reposed in the limousine parked in the basement garage, I was in no mood to cope with a tough shield.

"Listen, Citizen, I got 4,000 units tucked away in the Imperial Demaratus Security Trust, an' it's yours if you just let me get up. I'll buzz out of here—you'll never see me again, and I mean it! I don't know nothing, honest to Holy Vuudhana, I don't."

His voice was high and nasal and raw with desperation. I dug a cold steely stare into his frightened eyes and his voice died away. He stared back at my gaze. And he didn't like what he thought he saw there.

"You got a name?" My voice was level and hard.

He licked his lips, eager to please.

"S-sure I got a name! Brodvig, Wilm Brodvig! I . . ."

"Who do you work for?" My flat voice cut across his eager whimper like a whiplash across soft flesh.

"Why—Kory—Kory Henders."

A few more questions brought out the data that this Henders was the taller of the two men who had gotten out of the limousine when it grounded; the one who had snarled at the fat man when under my partial control he had acted so dazed. I had gunned down Henders and one other thug of his small gang, named Ogstrum, before escaping in the stolen limousine, you may remember.

But this question-and-answer routine was taking too long and I would be here all night at this rate. I decided to probe.

I threw him into a slight trance, and he opened up like a boiled oyster.

For the next twenty minutes or so I riffled through his memory and picked what passed for his brains with great ease but to little avail. He was a simple thug, up for hire to anybody and certainly no insider. In fact, most disappointingly, he proved to be a local skapper as I had guessed, hired only that morning by the fat man, Dom—he didn't know the rest of his name, of course. Dom had hired him, and the two other thugs I had rayed down, for a simple snatch-job. No, he didn't know who I was or why Dom wanted me. All he knew is that they—Dom and his group—knew where I was, *i.e.*, at the Association headquarters. They put Dom down to wait for me to come out of the building into the parking lot, where Dom was going to trap me in the tangle-field and stungun me. They had remained aloft in the rented limousine and were to stay up until Dom signalled or there was trouble.

And, no, he didn't know where they were to take me after Dom grabbed me. Dom gave them their instructions piece-meal, one bit at a time.

In other words, he didn't know anything that was of the slightest use to me. I could have guessed it all. The thugs had the look of local talent about them from the first glimpse I had had of them. I contemplated him sourly, wishing I had blown off his head instead of Dom's. Obviously, it was the fat little man who had belonged to the Opposition. He had been staked out in Demaratus Station waiting for my arrival. When I came in the terminal, he knew I was the one he was looking for. He came down in the shuttle with me and hired the three skappers knowing exactly where they could find me later.

Cold fingers were crawling up my spine. *How* had Dom known who I was? Surely, I had no enemies, not in the whole bloody galaxy! I knew this for a fact. I had been out of circulation for a century and a half. The average human lifespan, in these days of KLN-suppressants and hormone-booster treatments, was still hardly more than a hundred sixty, maybe a hundred seventy years. How could I have any enemies? One nice thing about being an immortal—if you just wait long enough, all your enemies die off. Anybody still around who was my foe back when I ran Citadel, why, hell, he would have been just a kid, twenty at the most! *Something was wrong, very, very wrong. This just didn't make any sense!*

So as I said, twenty minutes sufficed to pump Brodvig bone-dry of information. The little fat man had paid them in cash—ten thousand units—which, considering the amazing wad of money he still had left in the pocket of his japon when I searched him, added up to one small bit of information. The Opposition had a lot of operating capital. This was something big-time I had stumbled into the middle of, that was obvious.

And it was not a local outfit, either. Neither Brodvig nor his chief, Henders, had ever seen the little fat man before, Brodvig assured me. Henders had been puzzled as to how Dom knew where and how to get ahold of him, since he had never done a job for him before.

I could have given them the answer to that puzzle, since I knew Dom had been a telepath but I let it pass.

Well, I was through with Brodvig. Now to get him off my hands. No point in sending him off as a decoy, hoping the Opposition would want to find out from him what I had been up to, thus leading me to them. Dom had been running this end of the show alone or that's what all the indications added up to. I released his motor centers and dumped him out in the hall under post-hypnotic instructions to turn himself in at the nearest proctor station where I instructed him to confess to enough recent misdeeds to earn him a couple years' paid vacation on the Demaratus prison satellite.

But I erased from his memory everything having to do with myself. As far as Brodvig was concerned today just hadn't happened at all.

That took care of everything of immediate worry. Doubtless the management would find the corpse in the car but there was nothing to connect me with that case of suicide.

The only member of the Opposition around here was dead, so I didn't think there would be any more action that night. By this time it was 21:00 on the nose. Early enough—I could have caught the midnight shuttle to the Station and slept in my own bunk in *Wanderer* that night—but what the hell. It had been a long day, and busier than most, and I was tired. I decided to spend the night in the hotel and leave the planet tomorrow morning.

EIGHT

After breakfast in the dining salon, I checked out of the hotel and took a cab to the shuttle and thence back to Demaratus Station. I was on the alert every foot of the way but nothing happened to arouse my suspicions.

You see, I had remembered something that had slipped my mind the night before, what with all the unaccustomed excitement. While the cab was running me over to the Association building, *Wanderer* had reported being probed electronically by some men in a gig. That meant Dom had some friends around, unless these other men were local hired talent, too.

While the shuttle was taking me up to the terminal, I called *Wanderer* for further details on the precise nature of the probe to which the Opposition gig had subjected him. He replied they had felt out his energy shield and tried his spacedoor locking system with one of those high-speed electronic keys that broadcasts a speeded-up number series hoping to hit on the precise code that releases the locks. Since the ship thedomin operates the spacedoors and opens only to me personally, the electronic key did nothing.

"Did they try anything else?"

"Yes, one thing more," the ship replied through the little transceiver surgically buried in the mastoid bone of my skull. "They studied me through an alphascope."

"Did you repel the scope?"

"No, I permitted it free access."

73

I cancelled the transmission. This was interesting news, and maybe it added up to something. An alpha-scope detects the proximity of a human being—of any sentient being, actually, except for robotic, crystalloid or thedominic sentience. It is sensitive to the alpha wave broadcast by the brain—sort of a long-distance electroencephalograph which is also sensitive to alpha emissions. And this could only mean the Opposition was trying to find out if I had left anybody in charge of the ship.

We were pulling into the shuttle bay. I shot another call to my ship.

"*Wanderer*, there's a chance someone may attempt my capture as I approach you. Do you detect any vehicular action in your immediate vicinity?"

His answer came in a moment. "There are several scooters and two cargo vans operating within a radius of one thousand yards of my position and several ships moored nearby are partially manned."

"Yes, but anything suspicious?"

A silence. Then:

"There is one gig in parking orbit just beyond the fringe of my energy shield. I did not notice it before because it is hidden behind a 360° light-baffle. I am monitoring it on the asdar screen now. Asdar reports the spacedoors are open and several men are nearby in airsuits. I would judge their activities as definitely suspicious."

So would I. An invisible gig with men hovering about. Beautiful!

"Thanks, *Wanderer*! Now hear this! Special operating procedures follow, which supercede your standard operating procedures in categories C through H and the entire K series: these men will probably try to capture or at least attack me as I approach. They will most likely wait until you bring down your

74

energy shield so as to permit me entry into your spacedoor. You will not interfere in any manner unless, and until, you detect deployment of energy weapons. This procedure does not include use of a neuronic scrambler. Repeat, do not fight back if I am attacked with a neuronic scrambler, unless I am subjected to same for a period of time sufficient to kill. As soon as I cease this transmission I will leave the transceiver on so that it emits a carrier wave. When, and if, my captors transport me either to planet Demaratus, to another orbital station, or off-planet and into paraspace, you will request departure clearance from the Docking Authority in normal manner and track my wave, following at a distance beyond reach of their detectors. You will continue to track me wherever I am taken and will maintain a posture of armed readiness, prepared to get me out if I call for help or if my wave should for any reason cease transmission. Understood?"

"I understand and will comply."

"Transmission ends. Now."

Maybe I was taking a big chance by letting the Opposition ambush me this way but sometimes you have to risk it. Sure, I could have fought back in hopes of grabbing a prisoner who could tell me what I wanted to know about the Opposition. But that might have ended in another stalemate. I fought back when Kory's gang tried to grab me back there in the parking lot and such was my luck that the one single prisoner I took hardly knew anything.

You will understand that before I could effectively employ counter-actions against the Opposition, I had to find out just who they were and what they wanted with me. Until I discovered the answers to those questions, I was flying through space blind with my asdar nonfunctional.

I had already done some thinking about who the Opposition might possibly be, although I had little enough data in the banks to expect a valid extrapolation. For one, this might conceivably be the long-delayed culmination of a century-old private vendetta. I've already mentioned how unlikely it was that I could have a personal enemy still living but it was fully possible that the *children* of some foe from the good old days was trying to wreak a spot of vengeance for some ancient wrong. If so, his or her grievance would have to date back to before Year 3962 of the Imperium, which was when I turned Citadel command over to Ben Dalmers and I couldn't think of anything around that date that could have resulted in a vendetta of this tenacity and intricacy.

Of course, I came briefly out of retirement just about a hundred years ago but that was to handle an outbreak of Dirghama and I'm sure I made no enemies then.

Another possibility had also occurred to me. Suppose Dom and his compatriots were actually agents of the Intruder—either traitors enlisted through subversion or flesh robots infiltrating our society from the Magellanics? This seemed mighty possible and was by far the grimmer of the two alternatives. And then again, come to think of it, there was a faint possibility that this was a case of mistaken identity and had nothing to do with the Intruder at all. That is, maybe some gang was out to pull a really big job of some kind on Demaratus and had planted Dom in the terminal to watchdog for any telepathic practor who might turn up on the trail of this plot. Spotting me, Dom might have panicked and jumped to the conclusion that my arrival at just this time was involved with their plot, whatever it might be. Anyway, I had to find out. And the quickest way to discover what they wanted with me was to let them have me. So I went about my business just as if I did not know that a trap was already laid for me.

I got off the shuttle, processed through outgoing customs again, turned in my Demaratan credit card, picked up my scooter, donned my airsuit and zepped out to where *Wanderer* was parked. This time I was ready for the attack and had taken all the precautions I could. The Opposition had no way of guessing that *Wanderer* was anything more that just an ordinary cruiser with extra-heavy shielding and a pick-proof lock. They knew I had no confederate aboard who could fight back when I fell under their attack. It must have looked as easy as easy can be.

Sure enough, when I halted the scooter and *Wanderer* dropped his screens to let me aboard, they jumped me. I didn't feel like being stungunned again, so en route I had tinkered with my mindlock and made it opaque to the frequency of a neuronic weapon. There was no way they could detect this.

They caught me in the crossfire of three stunguns and I flopped realistically. It's a good thing the scooter had a safety belt or I might have gone floating down into the clutches of the planet's gravitational field. That would have been a fine way for a Star class telepath to end up—as a meteorite!

Wearing full light-baffles, they grabbed me and the scooter and bundled us aboard the invisible gig. I had been half-afraid they would try to board *Wanderer*. One look at his interior and they would know he was no ordinary ship. And there was a damn good chance they might try it because Docking Administration would soon begin to wonder why my ship was still moored at Demaratus Station when I had already processed through outgoing customs.

But the gig wasted no time in entering the cargo

77

hold of a nondescript freighter moored no great distance away. The spacedoors were sealed behind us and I guessed—correctly—that we were bound off-planet immediately. Obviously, they couldn't be bothered burdening themselves with another ship. Let Docking Administration wonder all it liked, there would be nothing to connect my disappearance with the departure of the freighter. Dozens of spacecraft of all kinds were arriving and departing every hour. Demaratan proctors would have no reason to suspect one ordinary freighter.

Once aboard, they turned off the light-baffles and secured the gig for a quick departure. Using my sensories I took a good look around. The cargo hold was empty—empty of cargo, that is. In fact, the cargo bays had been torn out and the whole compartment newly outfitted with mooring cradles. And these cradles accommodated a broad variety of auxiliary spacecraft. They held everything from scooters and an extra gig to crawlers and atmospheric skimmers. There was even one four-man scout capable of orbit-to-surface operations very elaborately camouflaged as an ordinary aircar.

This freighter was, in effect, a regular spacecraft-carrier nesting a small private fleet! I was impressed. And mighty curious.

Having gotten a good look around, I now turned my attentions to the gang who had ambushed me. They were eight in all and I had never seen any of them before. They were a tough-looking crew with hard faces and vicious eyes. And they looked like ordinary gunmen of the sort any mastermind can hire by the dozen for a big job off-planet. I didn't see any among the eight with the pale, washed-out complexions of Demaratans and that made me feel good. I guess my gamble was worth the risk after all; these were probably full-fledged members of the Opposition. The gang seemed to have been recruited mostly from the Hercules worlds. There were a couple big, raw-boned men among them, obviously terrestrials of colonial stock; a couple of swarthy renegades from Arkonna with beards dyed indigo; a number of scruffy, mean-looking natives for the Rilké, Chahuna or Faftol clans; at least one Nomad from the Veil and a blond, dull-eyed Centaurian. The only nonhominid among them I could see was a sleek-furred Catman from Kermnus, a low-caste Sss'tuurl from the patterns dyed in his furred upper arms.

They stripped off my airsuit and removed my gunbelt. One of them turned off my mindlock and went through my pockets, taking everything but my half-used pack of aromatiques which he most unwisely did not even bother to examine. They grinned and joked when they found the huge wad of cash I had lifted from Dom. Another of them scrutinized my rings and then pulled them off and added them to the little pile of loot. Then they ran a portable scanner over me from head to foot. It was only tuned to detect ferrous metals, so they found nothing.

The one who seemed to be the leader of the ambush gang was a small, wiry, middle-aged Herculian of about seventy. He had sharp, mean little eyes and a hungry look and his lean jaws were pockmarked from a bout with Blacklands fever. He had the Web Stars written all over him and the back-alleys of Argain were in the nasal whine of his voice.

While I was being searched, he went over to a wallphone.

"Commo, let me have the boss," he grunted. A momentary pause, then, "Boss? This is Kile, down in

79

Cargo. We got him easy, no problem. You wanna look him over before we zepp him in with the other one? Right!"

He turned to snarl, "Look alert, you guys, the boss is coming down with the med to have a look."

The other one, I thought. *Does that mean they have another prisoner?*

A couple of minutes later two men stepped out of the gravity well that connected with the upper decks. One was obviously "the med," a bony little man with a medikit clutched in one hand. And the other was, beyond question, the "Boss." He was a big man, well-fleshed and had about him that hearty, jovial air of a moneyed man of position—the aura of expensive jewelry, beefsteaks and brandy, luxury hotels and costly pleasures. But the illusion of joviality was a lie. One look at his hard, heavy face and cold eyes told you that. The wiry little ambush-leader, Kile, met him and his companion at the well with a cringing, servile demeanor and ushered the two over to where I lay. They had finished searching me by now. Carelessly, they had left me wearing my own space-fatigues. Either they were confident of their ability to hold me, or the scanner-test persuaded them I had no gadgetry concealed on my person. In either case, they were acting like amateurs because they left me in full possession of a micro-miniaturized arsenal—for what seemed to be an ordinary, innocent set of airsuit liner coveralls was one of my special "business" suits.

They would have been smart to strip me to the buff and give me some cast-off clothing to wear. That they didn't was a tactical error and I was determined they were going to regret it.

The boss raked me over with a cold, measuring glance and pawed contemptuously through the pile of belongings that they had found on me.

"Just junk, chief," Kile observed. The boss grunted, then waved forward the medic.

"Look him over. See when he's coming out of it," he said flatly. And I began to sweat. I could impersonate the victim of a stungun assault well enough to fool the eye—that just took a little acting. But a meditest was something else and the doctor probably had an e.e.g. in his kit. If he used that, he could tell instantly that I was faking because I could not disguise my amount of mental activity from an electroencephalograph.

Oddly enough—to my intense relief—he either didn't have one or didn't bother to use it if he did. He gave me a very brief once-over, too. The doctor was a scrawny old man of ninety or so, with the red-rimmed eyes and loose twitching mouth of a kelsenite-habituate.

As he bent down to examine me, I threw myself into a light trance state, the better to fake the affects of stungun paralysis. I was ready to seize control of his mind if he reached for a portable e.e.g., although using any of my T-powers beyond merely my sensories was risky and might be detected by another telepath, if they had one aboard.

But the old man gave me a most cursory examination. He checked my pulse, pushed back my upper lid and flashed a narrow light-beam into my eye and then got up stiffly.

"Well?" the boss demanded.

Apparently my hastily-assumed trance fooled the medic for he reported in a quavering voice, "The patient seems to have sustained only a glancing shot and should be coming out of the mental paralysis at any moment."

Kile's swarthy face flushed at the implied criticism of his gang's marksmanship.

81

"Chief," he said indignantly, "I swear t'Plenum we had three beams on him! Why, at fifty yards my boys c'd—"

Just at that moment my sensories detected an audio-beam transmission from somewhere very close by.

I wasn't attuned for reception but I managed to catch the "peaks" of the beam. What I heard made utterly no sense to me—then. It was a jumble of syllables that sounded like "GEERPTSFOOMENELG-TIVTEEEFF." I filed the nonsense word away for for further study later. Meanwhile, things were moving forward swiftly.

The boss had not been listening to Kile's indignant protestation. His attention was elsewhere. Now he waved the little gang-boss into silence and turned a wide, expansive grin on the gunmen who stood around apprehensively.

"Doesn't matter. You got him, that's the important thing. Good work, boys! I'll put in a good word for you when I see the Big Boss. . . ."

I had been wondering what the big man reminded me of, with his well-fed, impassive face and cold, calculating eyes and general air of genial prosperity. He was fitted out in expensive yachting duds. Jewelled rings flashed on his well-manicured hands. He was wearing a very, very expensive mindlock. These things were obvious to the eye. But he had a homogenized look. I couldn't pin down his birth-world with any kind of accuracy at all. And, although he spoke Neoanglic with a slight trace of accent, he had one of those deep, rich, well-trained voices from which the overt regional flavor had been professionally removed, like a newscaster speaking on the deleo to a galaxy-wide audience.

He had the fleshy, prosperous look of an upper-echelon management executive about him, a sort of unconscious knowledge of his own power that accepted, without really noticing, the considerable deference the others, all lowly underlings, mere pawns, displayed towards him.

But when he turned with that expansive gesture, that beaming smile, that loud hearty voice that rang with false warmth and joviality, I suddenly had him tagged.

A politician, of course. What else?

Kile fairly wriggled with relief and pleasure. "Aw, that's big of you, boss. *Real* big! You know me an' the boys . . . anything we can do for the Big Boss . . . anytime, anyplace. . . ."

The boss gave another of those hearty, beaming smiles. I noticed that the warmth of his smiles did nothing to take the chill out of his hard cold little eyes. "I know that, Kile," he said firmly, "and, believe me, the Big Boss knows it too. And when *The Time* comes . . . well! . . . the Big Boss is gonna remember you and your boys. Yes, you'll be all set."

The "boys" grinned and nudged each other, exchanging bright glances.

"Now, boys," the boss went on loudly, "I gotta get back up to Command and get this tincan zeppin' along. Kile, you take our friend here and you lock him up real good and tight and we can get going. Put him in with the other Citadel agent we caught."

"Right, boss!"

He turned on his heel and strode swiftly and purposively over to one of the gravity wells, the med following behind him.

The *other* Citadel agent?

Now, that was something to think about.

I thought about it all the way to my cell.

NINE

Kile told a big lug with straw-blond hair and watery pale eyes to cart me off to the brig. From his looks and the breadth of his muscle-bound shoulders I figured he came from the heavy gravity planet, Strontame, and from the casual ease with which he tossed me over one shoulder I knew I was right.

The brig was up several decks from the cargo hold. Since there was now just the muscle-man and me, I risked some plain and fancy snooping with my primaries as we went up the gravity well. This way I spotted several entry ports and observation blisters that had been converted to gun emplacements. They were crowded with some of the heaviest ship-mounted laser batteries I had ever seen this side of a Fleet battlewagon.

Snooping the main drive compartment, I also observed some heavy-duty shield projectors jury-rigged on cargo dollies and spliced in to the central power core of the cold-fusion assembly. This so-called freighter had been carefully, and unobtrusively, converted into a medium-heavy battle cruiser. Why, from the armament and shielding I snooped, it probably had enough zazz to hold its own against a full squadron of Naval craft.

That was interesting, too. That kind of shielding is costly and you don't buy laser batteries of that weight with pin-money. The Opposition had money behind them. Real money. I had stumbled onto something a lot bigger than I had first estimated.

A surly-faced Narlionid with apricot skin and slant

85

eyes that glistened like oiled satinwood was standing guard over the brig lock, armed with a heavy Barringer. He and the big lug from Strontame exchanged a few words and as the Narlionid opened up I noticed with more than a slight qualm that a dampener field had been set up just outside the door, up against the wall. From the position of its cone-antenna I guessed it was set to cover the brig area. And this was mighty bad news. It meant that, once I was on the inside, I would not be able to use my T-powers in any way.

This was my last good chance to try for a takeover of the Opposition ship, as far as I could tell at that moment. Very shortly I would be immobilized, my T-powers useless. Right now, if I wanted to try it, I could strike down the Strontamian and the brig guard and make my play for the control center up forward. It was a long chance but once inside that brig there would not be another.

My mind quickly examined possible courses of action open to me. How many men were aboard, anyway? I had observed about twenty, so far. Unless the freighter had a thedomin installation—and I had seen nothing in the power room to indicate there was a thedomin aboard—it would take about thirty or forty men to run a tincan as big as this one. Add to that the gun-crews it would take to man those batteries I had snooped and it made a total of easily fifty men aboard, or more.

Fifty to one is not exactly what you would call comfortable odds to gamble your life against, even counting full unhampered use of my mind powers and the mini-arsenal I was wearing secreted in my space fatigues. Still, a man armed with the T-powers of a Star class mind can make like a one-man army under the right circumstances. And I always had the *Wan-*

derer to count on for emergency diversionary tactics. Once locked in that mind-proof cell, my T-powers counted null and I would not even be able to flash a call for *Wanderer*, since the little gadget planted in my skull is no ordinary communications device but a sort of booster for telepathic waves. The dampener field would cut off my contact with *Wanderer*.

Well, I weighed the pros and cons of taking action on the spot against waiting for a better chance later on, and came to my decision in—literally—less time than it takes to describe the cogitations.

I decided to let myself be brigged. I was tempted to make my play right then, I'll admit. But I chose to go along for the ride, in hopes of being carried straight to Opposition headquarters. It would be just my luck, if I grabbed control of the ship now, to find that the top command echelon aboard had been implanted with suicide-if-captured mechanisms which would leave me with nothing but a bunch of hired gunmen who were unlikely to be on the inside when it came to long-range plans and the identity of the Big Boss.

A better chance might be coming up—maybe during interrogation. Many were the interrogation sessions of yore I had turned into two-way reciprocals by probing the minds of the very guys who were trying to search mine! Besides, there was that "other" Citadel agent. An unknown quantity but likely to be on my side of the fence once he learned just who I was. And there was always *Wanderer*, the biggest of the several aces up my sleeve.

Which reminded me that *Wanderer* had been instructed to go into attack action if my carrier wave went off—which it would do within split seconds just as soon as the muscle-bound Strontamian carried my carcass inside that dampener field. I flashed a quick message to *Wanderer*, telling him what was about to happen and for the love of Space to hold his fire.

The lock was open by now and the Strontamian carted me inside and deposited me, ungently, on a wall bunk while the brig guard held his Barringer on the other captive. The moment I was carried through the penumbra of the field, my sensories went dead and I was as blind as any ordinary person with his eyes closed. The dampener field, by the way, is just one loud blare of subelectronic "noise" broadcast on the same frequency as thought-waves. All it does is to "blind" or "deafen" the mind's T-powers, stunning the nerve centers into temporary and self-induced aenesthesia. They turn themselves off as a protective reaction, just as you squint your eyes shut against an unexpected blaze of light. Nothing very sophisticated about the dampener field; it just works, that's all.

My eyes shut and limbs-slack, I continued playing 'possum, sprawled on the bunk. I heard the Strontamian go out the lock. I heard him growl "Company for you!" to the imprisoned Citadel agent. I heard the lock swing shut, the hydraulic cams engage and mesh. Then I heard quick footsteps crossing the brig to my side.

I opened my eyes and saw the prettiest face I'd seen in a hundred years staring down at me.

"But you're the girl on the shuttle," I said inanely, "the girl with the gorgeous legs—the girl in the, uh, shiny metal stuff, uh—"

"Glitterfoil?" she offered, looking down at her outfit. She was wearing the same costume as she had worn on the shuttle. Now it was dulled and disarranged but she was still lovely. The long, supple, tanned legs were still long, supple, and tanned. Her elaborate glistening coiffure was a mess now, though —its lacy sculpture wrecked.

She certainly was a feast for hungry eyes even in her mussed-up state. Her eye makeup was exotic, with the pupils tatooed ruby, and the sleek planes of her face shimmered opalescent with glowpaint. Under all the high-fashion gunk, she had a good face with a pert little nose that owed nothing to homosculpt techniques and a jaw both deliciously small and delightfully stubborn. Her mouth was as warm and soft and wide, as pink and lucious as the inside of a ripe watermelon. And her skimpy three-piece costume of what she called glitterfoil displayed with admirable candor a pantherslim but adequately rounded figure. She looked about 24; I later learned she was 22.

"If you've finished admiring the view," she said coolly, "just who the Plenum *are* you?"

I grinned unashamedly. "Lady, pardon the eyes, but—well, they just didn't build Citadel Members according to such specifications back in my day!" Her eyes widened at this. She sucked in her breath.

"Th-they *said* they were going to grab somebody else from the Citadel," she said, and her voice was a little uneven as she spoke, "but I—I thought *I* was the only agent working on this case!"

I couldn't get that grin off my face. I said, "Lady, you probably are! I'm not really on this, uh, this 'case' at all. I just sorta stumbled into the middle of it. . . ."

"But I don't understand. You are from the Citadel, aren't you?"

My grin started to slip a little but I put it back where it had been. "Yes, from way back. My name is —Saul Everest."

She summoned up the ghost of a smile. "Meade Jarinth, Cn. Everest."

"Saul," I said. She nodded. My smile was getting tired, so I put it away for awhile. She continued:

"But if the Citadel didn't assign you to this, why are you here?"

It was a reasonable question. "In the first place, Meade, are we talking about the same case? That thing out there beyond the Rim?"

She nodded. "Of course! I came here to consult the records of the Rim Star Astronomical Association, to see if a visual confirmation could be found. What about you, Saul?"

"Same thing. I've been studying the galaxy's magnetic field, hobby of mine, and spotted the kind of perturbations it would take a rogue star to cause."

"Or a mobile planet," she said grimly. I nodded mutely.

"Then you weren't actually assigned to this one?" she pursued. I told her I was here on my own and that Citadel did not even know where I was right now. That seemed to depress her.

"Well, Citadel knows where I am," she said a bit glumly. "I got captured almost as soon as I landed from the shuttle—the moment I caught a cab. And when they let me know, a while later, that they were on the trail of *another* Citadel agent, I was hoping my actions had either been monitored or Citadel was backing me up with another agent on a duplicate mission. I was hoping you would crack this gang and get me out."

"And, instead, I got myself captured too," I said sympathetically. "Bad luck all around, Meade! Well, maybe we can still count on a rescue mission being sent out from Base once it dawns on the Grand Admiral that you aren't making your twice-a-day report."

Her wide eyes sparkled with something very like hope.

90

"I'd forgotten about that! Do you think the Grand Admiral will decide it's worth a full mission?"

I shrugged. "Can't say. But that's what the twice-a-day is for, isn't it? To give Base knowledge of the capture of any agent on assignment within six hours?"

She nodded. "Maybe we'll get out of this after all," she said brightly.

"Maybe," I grunted. I wasn't feeling too sure.

Well, this was all most interesting. But in the meanwhile we were prisoners of an unknown Opposition zepping through paraspace for an unknown objective.

Prisoners pass the time of their captivity any way they can. The brig was outfitted with an autochef, so I dialled myself a good lunch and talked with the girl for awhile. I decided not to waste my time inquiring as to which Citadel bureau she belonged, or who her immediate superiors were or her instructions. For one thing, the Opposition doubtless had the brig tapped under surveillance. I got a confirmation of this hunch very soon.

After finishing my meal I took a brief nap or what must have looked like a nap. Actually I was testing the dampener. Dampener fields have been in use for three or four millennia and I have occasionally encountered one here and there that was not quite watertight. There are six counter-lapse circuits in the innards of a field projector that have to be functional to 83% or you get areas where the blare of white noise from two components match and cancel each other out, leaving "holes" through which a good telepath can punch a probe without too much trouble. I was hoping to find this was one of those happy occasionals. It wasn't, so I gave up after awhile and slept, letting my phoney nap slide over into a real one.

I woke at the touch of a hand on my cheek. Meade

was bending over me. As soon as she saw I was awake she brightly asked if I had enjoyed a good nap. As she chattered this, she tucked a note pad in the chest pocket of my fatigues shielding the action with her body.

I yawned and stretched and said something to the effect that I had slept in worse places than this and by the way, did this brig have a 'fresher?

As I asked this, I casually let my eyes roam over the ceiling. Meade had presumably been locked in here long enough to have spotted whatever surveillance gadgetry had been installed for snooping on prisoners and from the angle of her body as she had masked her action of slipping me the note, I traced an invisible line to the ceiling and found without much trouble the unobtrusive spy eye planted high up on the further wall.

She indicated the whereabouts of the sanitary facilities and I ambled in. I wouldn't put it past the Opposition to plant a spy eye even in the john, so I examined my face in the mirror over the wash basin, checking on the patch-up job I had done on yesterday's bruises. While craning my head about to explore my face, I checked the reflected image of the walls and found two small eyes.

I stripped and used the refresher booth, palming the notepad as I bundled up my airsuit liner. Trusting that the detergent fog would obscure whatever surveillance equipment was planted in the 'fresher booth, I read the note scribbled on the top sheet of the pad. It was short and to the point.

4 SPY EYES PLANTED IN MAIN BRIG CABIN AND THREE IN 'FRESHER, it read. CONSTANT AUDIO TAP MAINTAINED DAY AND NIGHT, SO KEEP CONVERSATION TO GENERALITIES AND AVOID GIVING AWAY

INFO ON CITADEL. HAVE YOU ANY ACES UP SLEEVE? HOPE SO, BECAUSE I HAVE URGENT TOP PRIORITY 'MAYDAY' REPORT FOR CITADEL THAT MUST GET THROUGH INSTANTLY! CAN WE ESCAPE??? COMMAND OF THIS SHIP CONSISTS OF FLESH ROBOTS—AGENTS OF INTRUDER PLANET FROM MAGELLANICS WHO PLAN TO INFILTRATE NAVAL COMMAND, SUBVERT KEY INSTALLATIONS AND PARALYZE DEFENSES IN PREP. FOR ARRIVAL OF INVASION FLEET. CAN WE GET OUT OF HERE NOW???

This last sentence was heavily underscored. I balled the note up in the palm of one hand and let it flush through the floor grill when I rinsed off. Then I dressed and left the cubicle.

"Feel better now?" Meade asked.

I grinned and tipped her a slight wink. Stressing the last word ever so slightly, I said, cheerfully, "The answer to your question is yes."

She got it.

They had taken my timer when they went through my suit, so I asked if she had any idea what time it was.

"Oh, 13:00, maybe 14:00 Local," she answered. Too early in the day to try anything, I decided. Wiser to wait till night when most of the gunmen aboard would be in dreamland.

We passed the time in desultory conversation, waiting for evening. In the course of the chit-chat I got across to her the idea that we could break out and that I could get in touch with Citadel.

While we were having a light dinner that evening, courtesy of the local autochef, the freighter converted from paraspace to normal and proceeded on secondary

93

drive. This meant we were getting close to our destination, whatever it was. I dearly wished to stay aboard, in hopes of learning some important information during the interrogation periods that would doubtless follow upon our arrival at gang headquarters—presuming that's where we *were* bound.

But Meade was determined to make a break and contact Citadel as soon as possible. I was of another mind about this—having gone to all this trouble to get myself captured, it seemed pretty silly to try for an escape now, before I had learned where the Opposition base was, or had an estimate of their strength, or some detailed schedule of their future plans. But Meade insisted on the urgency of her information, so I decided to play along with her and escape, although it bothered the hell out of me to let myself be coerced into making what I was fairly certain was the wrong move. It sure was.

TEN

We pretended to turn in about 22:00. Privacy is impossible under the conditions of such close confinement, so this gave us a good excuse for sleeping in our clothes.

As soon as I had turned the lights out, I went into action. Since the freighter had no thedomin, the job of watching the screens on the other end of the spy eyes in the brig would be handled by men. And pretty thoroughly bored men they would be by now, too, for I had been careful that nothing whatsoever of any interest to them had happened in the brig all day.

Whoever was monitoring our words and actions would be pretty dull-eyed by now, having watched two people spend the day napping, exchanging listless chatter about books and deleo productions and just sprawling around on bunks. By this time, only a fraction of his attention would be on us and his reaction time would be slower than usual.

Now, the very fact that we were able to turn out the ceiling illuminant at all meant that the spy eyes were equipped to scan in infrared. But there would very likely be a time lag of a couple of seconds between the moment I snapped off the ceiling light and the bored, listless guard on the other end reached out and made the adjustment that switched his scanner from the octave of visible light to the infrared.

And I was counting on those couple of seconds.

When I snapped off the illuminants, instead of returning to my bunk I went over beside the entrance lock and put my left bootheel flat against the wall about two feet up from deck-level at the approximate height of the dampener field projector which stood on the other side of the compartment wall. The inner layer of this particular boot was printed microcircuits connected to an energy cell hidden in the bootheel. This miniaturized gadget projected a powerful electromagnetic field when turned on. And right now that magnetic field was tying the dampener's electronic guts in knots.

The field cut off dead on the very instant, just as I had figured it would. And my mind was free, alive, undeadened by the dampener. Unless you are a telepath yourself, you can never know what mind-dulling, brain-fogging torment the field inflicts on one with telepathic awareness. Imagine a brilliant, witty, articulate poet suddenly struck down with semantic aphasia, a great violinist suddenly struck absolutely tone-deaf, a pictorial artist gone stone blind. And you'll get some inkling of the deadening, leaden pall of the inhibiting force.

But now it was off—and my mind was free! It felt good; it felt beautiful. Like standing washed in rich golden sunlight after hours spent locked in a dark, tight, airless closet. Or like drinking in great lungfuls of tangy fresh air in wide-open fields, after starving on a subsistence-level trickle of stale, canned and reprocessed air from a suit compressor for dreary hours. It felt *wonderful*.

But I certainly didn't have the spare time just then to waste reveling in my new mental freedom. I had a shipful of enemies to kill or escape from and every passing microsecond brought us closer and closer to danger.

I slammed a probe deep in the brain of that guard who lounged sleepy and inattentive in a chair in the hall just outside the brig. Happily, he was not shielded by a mindlock. Not that it would have really made much of a difference, such was the brutal force with which I rammed that powerful probe viciously into the tenuous web of his neural connections.

He was not the same apricot-skinned Narlionid who had held this post when they lugged me in. Guard-shift must have changed during the intervening hours—not that it really mattered. The new guard, a big blond Centaurian with a scarred face and dull blue eyes, succumbed to my probe without time to make any resistance. I seized control of his central motor nerves and brought him off his butt and onto his feet double-quick.

In no time flat he had the lock open and we piled out into the corridor. Luckily, nobody seemed to be about at this hour or at least the hall was vacant as far as we could see or my sensories could probe. While the dumb Centaurian lug fumbled the brig lock shut and secure behind us, I relieved him of his hand-laser and picked his brains for a quick résumé of guard positions and patroled routes between this spot and the cargo hold, if any.

There were none, as it turned out. The gang might be great hands at a snatch but they were lousy when it came to their internal ship security. But this was all the better for me and the girl, of course.

With a print of the information in my mind, I sat the dull-eyed oaf down in his chair and put him to sleep with orders to stay deep in slumberland for a good hour.

Then we ran for it.

We were lucky. What with all the cubicles and cabins and intersecting corridors we had to pass, we only encountered one lone member of the Opposition on our trip between the brig and the gravity well that led to the cargo hold where the auxiliary craft were moored.

And this fellow—a surly-faced, fat-gutted Astaretha with the plum-purple skin and weird yellow pupils of his kind, a neuronic whip tucked into the sash around his middle and his ritual cap worn far back on his bald, glistening skull—he was a pushover.

His eyes goggled in wide astonishment when he saw us sprinting madly down the corridor towards where he stood. And his thick-lipped and sensuous mouth widened, too, but soundlessly. Before he had time to give voice to a shout or to even think of the neuronic weapon thrust through his gaudy, low-caste sash, I rammed my way into his amazed mind, grabbed his consciousness-center and put him to sleep even before his collapsing body could slap against the deck plates.

By the time the girl and I had reached the lip of the gravity well and jumped into it, the jig was up and alarm signals were flashing and klaxons were whooping all over the ship. I guess the bored guard stationed at the scanners had finally switched his scopes to infrared and saw we just weren't there.

We went down the well tube at breakneck speed and hit the cargo deck at bruising velocity. Half a dozen men were yelling and pelting for us. I took care of them one after another, just as fast as I could thrust a probe into their minds.

It was a sloppy escape, not up to my usual standards at all. We grabbed the first thing we saw that could handle itself in deep space, a gig like the one I had been brought here in. While sealing the gig and activating the controls I sent a probe questing for somebody near enough to the control board to operate the spacedoors for us. I found one, a gawky, middle-aged Micran who was staring at us across the hold incredulously. I seized his mind and in seconds the vacuum alarm sent guards scurrying for airtight cover. I didn't bother waiting for a clear hold, of course. As far as I was concerned, the whole bloody crew could eat space. The doors yawned open and we went crashing out of the cradle and were spaceborne in less time than it takes for me to tell of it.

Blackness was all around us, broken by the cold dead glitter of the stars. Everything was happening at once; there was no time for thought. Meade clung to a stanchion, white-faced and gagging as her stomach rebelled to the suddenness with which it had been thrust from the comfortable .90% gee of the freighter's artificial gravity to the free fall of the gig, whose mass was too slight to sustain the luxury of an artificial gravity field.

"Get into one of these suits. Come on, hop to it, girl!" I yelled, leaning from the console to grab one off its rack for myself, tossing another to her. She gasped like a beached fish, looking as if she was going to lose her dinner at any moment.

"Come on, *move*," I growled. "Forget your gut. It's all in your mind anyway, you know. And you'll be in worse trouble if they blast us and rupture our hull . . ."

I struggled into my own suit, cursing the cramped quarters, trying to keep one hand on the controls and one eye on the scopes as I did so. Glancing back, I saw that Meade was halfway into her suit. She had released her hold on the stanchion and was kicking her way into the legs while turning over and over in mid-air. Considering the condition of her three-piece outfit, I got an eyeful of an awful lot of slim tanned leg.

The freighter was long since out of sight. Even

99

on seconadry drive, and at cruising speed, she had dwindled and vanished in the black void like a hurtling rifle bullet. Closing the helmet and testing suit circuits, I peered fiercely around at the screens, trying to get an idea of where we were, roughly. I spotted a couple of Cepheid variables among the starclouds strewn across space to port but there was no time to count their frequency and, maybe, identify them. I dialed the magnification way up and spotted S Doradus unmistakably. That gave me a crude orientation. I kicked the gig around in a sharp curve and slammed down on the pedals.

We had a chance, a mighty slim one, of losing the freighter. When we left the cargo hold we were traveling at a right angle to the freighter's path. It had been flying a straight vector and as we were now in normal space and the familiar Newtonian laws were in force again, it would take that fat bucket of bolts an appreciable period of time to kill forward momentum and drag all that inertia around to double back on its trail. By that time we had a good chance to avoid being located. It is rather difficult to locate *any-thing* in deep space. Old-fashioned radar systems don't work very well because the distances involved are just too great and a radar beam spreads out and disperses too soon for any sort of hard, accurate sighting. Asdar—technicalese for "All-Spectrum-Detecting-And-Ranging"—is completely different from the old-fashioned radar early ships used. Asdar "reads" radiation—it can be tuned to "see" in any octave of the electromagnetic spectrum, all the way from the slow wavelengths of power generation up through the constantly narrowing wavelengths of radio waves, infrared, visible light, UV, x-rays, to gamma, cosmics and transcosmics. Any sort of radiant energy paints a picture on the asdar scope and distance doesn't matter. But the beam is narrow and it's mighty easy to sweep right past a tiny blip like our gig would make and miss it cleanly.

Even now they were turning. I couldn't see the freighter—it is only possible under very special circumstances for one ship to actually *see* another ship in space, distances and velocities are too great—but I was taking every evasive action I could think of to dodge their beam.

As it happened, they didn't even try to catch the gig on their screens. I should have remembered how thoroughly the Opposition had armed that phoney freighter. The laser batteries should have tipped me off—the ship was set up for close infighting. That meant they would be equipped with anti-personnel weapons.

They were.

A thrilling shock went through me. I threw back my head and yelled deafeningly in the confines of my airsuit helmet. An eerie effect took place throughout the cramped little cabin of the racing gig: violet light sprayed from the sharp corners of metal surfaces. Had we been unhelmeted, we would have sniffed the sharp metallic stench of raw ozone in the cabin's atmosphere. Then I slumped forward across the console, dimly conscious, arms and legs numb and useless.

"Saul—*Saul!*" A white, strained face gaping behind her glassy helmet. A slim, strong, young hand clutching at my shoulder. Miraculously, Meade had escaped the blast unharmed.

The anti-personnel field is the simplest of weapons: an electrical charge extruded on a broad, expanding wave-front, sweeping through space. Powerful enough to shock, to paralyze, to stun but not strong enough to kill. The blast had caught me full; strapped in the

101

naked steel frame of the pilot chair, my feet flat against steel deck-plates which acted as perfect conductors for the electrical charge.

But Meade had been floating in free-fall, struggling into her suit, not touching any metal which could act as a conductor. In effect, she had been perfectly "grounded" and the blast of the field had passed her by.

She struggled to pull me off the console.

A red light flashed on the board. I saw it through half-closed eyes. We were receiving an asdar beam. The freighter was slowing, maneuvering for the kill. Or the re-capture. It has been one hell of a lousy escape, all right—I knew I should've stayed in bed.

She was shaking me with desperate strength, her helmet against mine, yelling something. We had only seconds of freedom left. And I couldn't move; could hardly even think.

"Saul! Saul! They're pulling up to portside. I see a gig launching for us. Quick—*how can I get my message to Citadel!* Think, Saul, think! I must get through—I must get my information into the hands of the Grand Admiral. . . ."

Her words beat against my dull brain like waves pounding a great rock half-sunk in wet, thick sand. I strove to speak, to move numb lips.

"Deleo," I muttered.

"Yes?" Her voice was sharp, almost hysteric. "What setting? Saul! *What setting?*"

"Way up the dial . . . way past the commercial settings. . . ."

She shook me again, trying to keep me awake. My head lolled loosely, drunkenly. All I wanted to do was sleep.

"177—"

"Yes? *Hurry.*"

"177—point—98071 . . . mus' be precise . . . un-nerstan'?" I mumbled through cold, tingling lips.

She nodded determinedly. "Yes. I understand, Saul. 177.98071 and the setting must be precise. Right. Sleep now, Saul."

She let my head fall back against the console.

Then she took from my belt the hand laser I had grabbed from the big Centaurian brig guard. She steadied it with both of her small capable hands on the grip.

And she shot me. In the chest.

Her helmet was closed. She could not smell the frying fabric of the airsuit. Or the sweet, sickening stench of burning human flesh. But she could imagine the odor that filled the cramped space of the cabin and her nostrils went pinched and white and her lips pressed tight against the bile that flooded her mouth. In a moment she had her nausea under control.

Aiming with great care, she fired the pistol again and shot me through the brain.

Then she released her fingers and let the pistol float free.

She looked down at the fried, charred, blackened corpse. Her face was pale and set but there was no expression on it. No expression at all. Then she looked away and she did not look back again at my body.

She turned to the intercom and flicked the phone switch.

"I got it," she said quietly.

The hearty jovial voice of the boss filled the cabin.

"Are you certain?" he asked.

She nodded coolly. Then, remembering this was just an audio rig and not a regular sight-and-sound phone, she said, "Yes. A deleocast setting on which an emergency call can be sent to Citadel headquarters."

103

The heavy warmth of the professional politico entered his voice. "Very well done, Cns. Jarinth! Very well done, indeed! With the proper setting we can phoney up an emergency call. We'll pretend the agent calling in is a dying man in too much pain to exchange any sort of verbal recognition codes. We'll have our man mumble something disjointedly. Doubtless, the Citadel people will ask him to repeat. They may ask for a repeat two or three times before cutting their beam. And that should give us enough time for the technical boys to tap and trace the beams and get a fix on their headquarters' location."

Her voice was cool, competent. "I thought it was scientifically impossible to get a position-fix on a deleocast beam," she remarked.

He chuckled, a thick, throaty sound.

"Not impossible—just very, very difficult and demanding some extremely expensive special equipment. Leave it to our technical staff. They'll have the Citadel base pinpointed on the charts by this time tomorrow!"

She nodded.."Fine. Now pick me up, will you?"

"Of course—leave your beam open. The gig will home in on your wave. Oh, by the way, was there any trouble with our impulsive and overly-trusting young friend?"

"None at all. He's dead," she said.

"Excellent, excellent! Again, Cns. Jarinth, my hearty congratulations on a job well done. You, ah, you are quite *certain* life is extinct?"

"Quite certain," she said flatly. "His brains are splattered all over the inside of the observation blister."

Five minutes later the second gig locked its magnetic grapnels on the first and matched intrinsic velocities so that Meade Jarinth could transfer from one cabin to the other.

Once she was aboard and the grapnels were detached, the second gig veered off on a wide vector and curved about heading for the open spacedoors of the freighter, which had matched velocities and was riding about twenty minutes' flight to port on a converging course with the stolen gig.

As soon as the recovery crew were aboard, the cargo spacedoors sealed and the gig moored safely in its cradle again, the freighter came about smartly and held the hurtling ovoid of the first gig steady in its scopes while the artillery crews used the small vehicle and the corpse that manned it a for a bit of target practice.

Moments later the gig was an immense ball of incandescence—and then, an expanding cloud of superheated gas that swelled, dimmed and dispersed against the thinness of the void.

The freighter kicked about and resumed the interrupted flight.

In a few seconds it was gone from sight and the cold dead glare of the stars could see it no longer.

ELEVEN

It took the freighter about an hour and a half flying time on its secondary drive to reach its destination.

This destination turned out to be a small terra-formed planetoid circling a blue-white Main Sequence star with a B5 spectrum, similar to Alpha Eridani—Achernar, to you—but somewhat smaller.

I did not recognize the star because clinging to the hull of the freighter through the magnetic field generated by the gadgetry concealed in my left boot, I did not have access to a spectrograph and had to use sight alone.

They put the freighter in parking orbit around this small planetoid which seemed to be the only body in orbit around this star. That is, the only one I could spot with the naked eye but it seemed a likely assumption to make. This was an expensively terraformed worldlet laid out in elaborate parks and gardens. It looked like the private estate of some lordling of the Imperium, maybe the retreat of a planetary hegemon or the hunting lodge of some grand muckedy-muck of the Centumvirate. Anyway, this was a luxury set-up not just a utilitarian gang base.

The Opposition ran everything under tight security wraps. So, undoubtedly, the Big Boss liked his privacy, too.

After a while the gig went down with eight persons aboard. I couldn't see exactly who they were, bundled in heavy airsuits, but probably the jovial politico was among them.

The gig made four trips, leaving a skeleton crew aboard.

I rode down with the last trip. My airsuit was not equipped with reaction pistols for extra-vehicular activity, so I could hardly land on the worldlet without hitching a ride. But there was no trouble about the trip and no danger of being seen. None of the eight thugs aboard was a telepath or wore a mindlock, so I just did what I had been doing ever since Meade shot me: if anybody looked in my direction, I insinuated a mental probe and cancelled out the visual memory. That meant, although they may have actually seen me, they did not remember having seen me. It was the next best thing to being invisible—which I would have preferred, but this suit was not fitted out with light-baffles.

The gig came down on a landing flat in the middle of an elaborate park full of tennis courts, swimming pools, *psi*-ball fields and conservatories. The conservatories were big glass structures serving as hothouses. The Big Boss, it seemed, bred rare *odontoglossums*. I hopped off as soon as the gig touched down and hid inside one of the conservatories. There is a limit, unfortunately, to the number of minds I can control at a time and to avoid accidentally being sighted by the ground crew clustered around the gig I got under cover as fast as possible.

The air inside the frosted glass dome was hot and humid and thick with perfume but I snapped open my face plate and doffed my suit, ignoring the thick sweet odor of half a hundred rare blossoms.

Up in front, by the temperature and humidity controls, I found some big lockers filled with specialized gardening tools. I stashed away my airsuit in one of these, hiding it well out of sight behind some fertilizer sacks. Then I went over to the further wall and took a good long look at the big house.

It was a regular mansion, built in an elaborate and stately imitation of the High Nemedrian style of architecture that had been popular among the wealthy and armigerous gentry five centuries earlier. It was very big. There must have been at least seventy rooms and the servant staff must have been as large as a small army.

It was virtually a palace. Nobody but a megalomaniac or a reigning hegemon would want to live in such grandiose surroundings. I began to get ideas about just what sort of a person the Big Boss was and of the kind of drives and ambitions that motivated him.

Things were beginning to fall into place. In fact, things had been adding up for me for several hours now. I had a pretty good idea of just what had been going on all this time.

"All this time" indeed! So much had happened so fast recently that it was difficult to realize that it had only been the day before yesterday that all of this began. But it was true. Only two days ago I had come home from a morning on horseback to get that call from R-2. It was incredible. It seemed like weeks had gone by but it was only two days since this thing started to roll. And in that rather small space of time I had been mind-probed while rubbernecking the window of a dress shop; almost ambushed while walking through a parking lot; forced to shoot my way out of a trap, ending up for the night in a luxury hotel with a fresh corpse stuck in the front seat of my car and a hot prisoner tied down in the living room; ambushed for a second time in mid-space; kidnapped aboard a private battleship disguised as a harmless freighter; locked up in a brig and forced to spend the evening with a beautiful girl and shot down and left for dead by said beautiful girl right smack in the middle of a vest-pocket-sized space battle. *Old buddy, you've had a busy weekend,* I thought to myself humorlessly.

Well, it was almost over. At least, I had hooked and crooked and finally persuaded the Opposition to carry me straight to their headquarters. A little snooping around and maybe a little bit more action and I call it a day.

If my luck held out.

Which it didn't.

Again, I found myself waiting for darkness to fall. There were an awful lot of windows in that modest-sized imitation palace across the *psi*-ball fields. All too many eyes could be peering out of them at any time. But with night, hopefully, the eyes might all be closed.

It was late afternoon, Local, when I had hitched that free ride down from orbit on back of the gig. The terraformed planetoid probably had no more or less normal number of hours in its planned and artificial day, or so I guessed and was banking on.

My gamble proved out. Sunset came, right on schedule. The west flared with spectacular crimson and I caught myself wondering what sort of powdered minerals in the atmosphere gave that sensational effect and how they kept 'em in suspension. I would like to have Home equipped with sunsets like this one. It was gorgeous.

The shades of night were falling fast. Pretty soon soft spots would be going on, lighting up the soaring walls of sculptured white and cream and grey stone. Now was the time to make my break.

Trusting that my space fatigues would pass casual

110

inspection as gardener's coveralls in this dim light, I left the conservatory and strolled with elaborate casualness around the gaming courts and flower beds, winding closer and closer towards the big house. To aid my deception, I carried a gardening tool slung over my shoulder like a rifle, held my head down and walked with a lazy, shuffling amble.

I found a wall with long windows, what we used to call "French windows" in the old days back on Earth, and I found a row of dense candlewood trees growing close to the house. I crept behind them, found an empty room and let myself in by the simple and time-honored expedient of smashing a pane of glass and reaching through to unlatch the window.

Once inside, I began searching with all my sensories. My mind could detect the presence of another mind and seize control of it easily; thus I did not find it very hard to make my way deeper and deeper into the house. Everyone that encountered me had the memory instantly erased from his mind.

I prowled cautiously through the ground floor of the mansion, being careful to search each room and corridor with full sensories before venturing into it. The big house was decorated expensively—luxuriously—and with exquisite taste. There were suites and apartments hung with gorgeous tapestries, including priceless examples of subtle Vruu Kophe work. The Vruu Kophe race had been killed off back in the Third Imperial War which had begun in the sixteenth year of the Empery of Uxorian I and ended in the fifth year of Arban IV. That was three and a half millennia ago and any examples of the gorgeous tapestry-art of the now-extinct arachnidian race were incredibly valuable and even more incredibly rare, which meant the chief of the Opposition was wealthy on the grand scale.

111

Then came a series of corridors whose walls were decorated with paintings, mullages, stabiles and chromophanes by the dozens—enough to stock three or four small museums. I recognized art by thirty or forty more famous artists of the past several centuries.

Wealthy was not quite the word.

Apparently, the ground floor of this palatial manse was for formal display, not for living. I passed through museum rooms and chambers given over to display cases of Herculean ivory, Baracheusian jewel carvings, Iocran wood sculpture, as well as enormous rooms filled with portraiture, statues and busts, mosaics, frescoes and curio collections. There was also a formal dining hall that could probably seat at a pinch two hundred guests, a ballroom big enough to house *Wanderer* and a library that you would have to see to believe. It must have held fifteen thousand books if it held a dozen, all rare first editions and fine bindings. Yes, I mean *real books*—genuine antiquities, printed on paper and bound between leather boards! —not just cassettes or tape reels, such as most people have been using for ages.

The Big Boss had real class, that was certain.

There must have been fifty guards stationed on the ground floor of this place alone, not counting the electronic surveillance equipment. I managed to dodge discovery without much trouble. I am an old hand at this sort of thing. (I've always thought I would have made a terrific cat burglar—it's an idea, you must admit.)

The sentient sentinels gave me little trouble. My sensories gave me advance warning whenever they came near and as none of them wore mindlocks, a bit of mental tampering made me just about discovery-proof. The ever-vigilant electronic guard system was a bit more difficult to circumvent. Once again,

I thanked my luck that the boys on the freighter had left me in possession of my "business" suit. Wired into the fabric of those fatigues and concealed in all sorts of unlikely places was enough microminiaturized gadgetry to fool the most complicated system of spy eyes, body-warmth detectors, proximity alarms, audio search beams and any other sophisticated mechanical watchdogs you could think of. I had a couple narrow escapes, I frankly admit, but I got through everything undetected.

The palace had two main wings which I searched after disposing of the central part of the structure. These wings were given over to business. And a pretty dubious business it would seem to be. I saw a communications set-up that would not have been shamed by comparison with Imperial Naval headquarters on Trelion V and a code room as fully equipped as Citadel itself.

Several suites were given over to operations and files. I didn't poke around in them very much, just gave them a quick once-over-lightly to ascertain their purpose. This was the heart and brain and nerve center of the Opposition's entire activities—whatever they were—and undoubtedly the electronic surveillance here would be pretty fierce. So I left these suites alone, just taking a look-see with my sensories.

I had no particular desire to trigger the self-destruct circuits presumably built into those files. If I wanted to attract attention, a far easier way would be to go outside and shoot up the grounds.

Finally, I began a tour of the upper floors. Here, one might guess, were the living quarters of the staff. Electronic safeguards should have been minimal on the second floor, where any sleep-walking Third Assistant Under-Chef or philandering Sub-Butler, Second Class, would be likely to trip off a proximity alarm or light up a body-warmth detector. Here I felt relatively safe and thought I could probably do a little snooping into sleeping minds.

I couldn't have been more wrong, as it turned out. I ran straight into a robot.

An ice-cold ball of lead congealed in the pit of my guts and my heart, as the ancient cliché has it, rose into my mouth. I froze motionless. But it was no good.

I stared at it and it stared back at me. Cold receptor lenses (equipped, I noted all in one flashing second, to scan in visible light and infrared both) subjected me to a searching scrutiny. When I realized that proximity and body-warmth detectors would not be used to keep the living quarters under surveillance, I should have known that anybody as rich as the museum-*cum*-art-gallery-*cum*-library on the ground floor exemplified, would be rich enough to afford a staff of robot watchdogs. They made perfect night watchmen. Tireless, unsleeping, ever-vigilant, they were guards you could not bribe, anesthetize, garrote, knock out, or fool.

Of course they were linked on a common circuit with the house thedomin, whose positronic memory retained the likenesses of every single sentient being or animal pet permitted access to the house. A single glance at any intruder, a microsecond for memory comparison with stored likenesses, and the robot guard could detect that intruder.

I barely got my body shields up in time to fend off the stungun bolt with which one of the forelimbs of the robot was equipped.

Of course, I had no gun. Meade had used it to shoot me with. And I hadn't thought it necessary to relieve any one of the guards I mind-controlled of his hardware in passing. I must admit I *did* feel kind of

114

naked without an iron on my hip but it was too late to worry about past regrets now. I was trapped.

There was no way I could fight this thing—it must have weighed half a ton even without the caterpillar treads (the robotic equivalent of being barefoot. To avoid undue noise during sleeping hours, this tin-plated watchdog rode a soundless hover-field).

And I couldn't take it over as I had its human counterparts on the floor below. The human mind and robotic intelligence are incompatible, unlike human-and-thedominic sentience. Already it had flashed an alarm to the house thedomin; such a reaction would have been instantaneous. By now every other robot in the house had gotten the message, if I was right about them being on a common circuit.

There was a chance, the slightest, slimmest chance possible, that I could get the house thedomin under the control of my mind. I had done it before, at various times in my lurid past. But no chance of riding the robot's beam back to the thedomin.

I was trapped, all right.

Before the neuronic attack ended, security gates were sliding out of the walls and cutting me off from the nearest exits. Even if I had relieved one of the guards of his hand laser or Barringer, or whatever, I couldn't have cut my way through these grills. They were made of what looked like collapsium -9 and I would need a nega-grav-mounted semiportable energy gun to get through that stuff.

And then in the next fraction of a second the gas hit me. It must have been piped along the ceilings with release cocks every few yards or so.

It was the kind you don't have to breathe. All it had to do was touch your skin and you were down for the long count. I didn't even feel the floor when it came up and slapped me in the face. . .

115

TWELVE

Well, there I was in this big comfortable pneumo upholstered in what felt like fine velour. The chair was fully equipped with miniature tangle-field projectors that held me in their molasses-like grip. My arms and legs were immobilized, and comfortable enough, except when I tried to move them. Then I felt the tingling quicksand feeling tighten over my limbs and the surface tension of the field felt like rough sandpaper as it dragged against my bare skin.

This time, I had been stripped completely naked, my body gone over with a fine-toothed comb, and then somebody had thoughtfully put a dressing gown over my nakedness.

They were through playing games, obviously.

The chair had just given me a jet of counteractive gunk and it withdrew its extensible hypospray from the big artery in my arm as I came awake. The effects of the gas were just about gone. I felt a little logy and heavy-lidded, and the gas had left a taste in the back of my mouth you could have scraped off my tonsils with a rusty butter knife, but otherwise, I felt chipper enough.

A nicely-focused and perfectly tuned dampener field was localized on my chair. I couldn't raise a watt of T-power if my life depended on it—which it probably did.

My chair sat in the middle of a long, high-ceilinged room decorated in exquisite taste. There were low tables of Kiogan and Mandrakor and Astysian work from the finest periods covered with expensive bric-abrac. Silver bowls filled with fresh-cut flowers added their sweetness to the cool air that blew from tangy woods beyond the tall windows. The carpeting underfoot had three-inch deep pile. The walls were beautifully paneled in rare woods, and here and there upon them hung still more paintings by famous artists, discreetly lit. The room breathed taste, elegance, luxury. And money. Lots of the latter.

Seated in a large, high-backed, wide-armed Kiogan chair across a low table from me, a slim, regal, beautifully-gowned and coiffured woman busied herself with tarrojan things of silver and fine crystal. The delicate aroma of excellent tarrojan rose to my nostrils.

"Good evening, Cn. Everest. Will you take nace or thoroway with your cup?" she inquired with a calm, gentle smile. Her hair, naturally grey, was built into an elaborate structure. Her gown, a long formal Tregephontane dining-robe, was made of dark rose velvet, silvery-grey silk and fabulously ancient lace, as yellow and fragile as old ivory. Her hands, slender and elegant and beautifully groomed, were without ornamentation except for one iridium ring that bore a Kyrian stardrop worth a quarter of a million units.

Well, she could afford it. And a dozen like it, out of the household money.

Of course, I knew her at a glance. Even hermitted away the past one hundred fifty years on Home, I had heard of her. You just don't get that rich, that powerful, without getting well known. To half the galaxy she was the saintly and martyred widow of a mighty statesman, cut down on the very threshhold of ultimate achievement; to these, the little people, she was a resigned, sweetly dignified widow, living in private seclusion. To the *other* half of the galaxy,

118

the rich, influential, titled, nobly born or ambitious, she was the reigning monarch of a powerful political machine who remained in seclusion, ready to return and claim her position of vast and central influence at any time, like the exiled queen of some fallen or deposed dynasty.

I will admit I was astonished to discover just who the Big Boss really was. Astonished? *Staggered* is, I think, the more appropriate word. The untouchable, pure, nobly-suffering paragon of wifehood . . . the bluest of the blue-bloods, the cream of the upper crust of Society . . . the Dowager Empress of good taste, good manners, and good breeding.

The biggest surprise, though, was to find her still alive. She had been an elderly woman way back in Year 3962 of the Imperium when I "retired." I had no idea just how old she really was but she must have spent a truly princely fortune on antigeriatrics, cosmetic surgery and longevity treatments.

"Thoroway, thank you, Madame Lyntonhurst," I replied quietly. "Although how I can drink it with my hands tied down I can't quite imagine. A long straw, perhaps?"

She smiled sweetly.

"That will not be necessary, Citizen," she said. Raising her voice just a little, she addressed the empty air. "I think Cn. Everest may be permitted the use of his hands, Control. But let us continue the restraint on his legs, just at present, if only to avoid accidents."

The tangle-fields projected from the arms of my pneumo went off and I rubbed my numb fingers together with relief. My several rings, I saw, had been removed. That was a pity. The Antares moon-opal on my pinky could have cut her in half with a needle-focussed laser beam, if I was still wearing it.

I half-wondered if she would be stupid enough to

hand me my cup but I should have known that no one as old or rich or powerful as Madame Lynton-hurst could have gotten as far as she had without having better sense than that. She poured my cup, slipped a sprig of thoroway into it and set it down on the edge of the table nearest to me.

"There we are, young man. I believe you can reach the cup from where you are without the necessity of getting up," she said, with a gracious, dreaming smile.

I could.

Sipping the fragrant brew of herbs, I remembered it had been a long time since I had eaten anything. The steaming decoction of spicy, mild tarrojan was deliciously pungent and tangy. I set the cup down and let my eyes drift around the perfectly appointed room.

"Nice place you have here," I remarked. "But then, I suppose, with all the annual dues of the Party to dip into, you can afford the good stuff."

She gave a silvery laugh and there was amusement in her well-bred, patrician voice as she said, "Come, now, young man. As you know, the funds of the Libertarian Party are devoted to purely political activities."

"Yeah. Spying, kidnapping, murder and building up a private Navy. I never did understand politics. . . ."

The polite, kindly expression on her fine-boned, aristocratic features did not alter by a millimeter.

"Now you are trying to insult me, Cn. Everest. As you must know, my husband, the late Centumvir, left me quite wealthy."

"Left you with a well-organized political party to play around with, as well," I said levelly. "He didn't pack half the units you inherited from your first three husbands."

Another gracious smile on that calm face.

"I see you are well acquainted with my history, young man. Unfortunately, I am not as familiar with your own. But, no doubt, we shall become better acquainted in time."

"No doubt," I grunted. "Especially if you go in for a bit of torture or like to drug your prisoners with a little monopentothal."

Another silvery tinkling laugh.

"I see you enjoy plain, honest talk, Citizen! Well, so do I."

"Yes, I believe in calling a spade a spade," I said lightly. "And a murdering, power-hungry old bitch a murdering, power-hungry old bitch!"

She lost just a bit of the sweet graciousness from her eyes and her gently smiling lips tightened and went just a trifle hard.

Just then a door opened across the room and Meade came in. A very different Meade from the bare-legged girl in the three-piece glitterfoil costume. She wore a modest, mousy tunic that covered her from collar-bone to knee-caps. Her hair was plainly dressed and her natural dark brown with fugitive red glints— no longer the fantastic sculptured and plasticined concoction ablaze with little witch-lights. No longer ruby red, her eyes were dark brown and subdued. The glowpaint had been washed away and a creamy tan, dusted with tomboy freckles, was revealed to sight. She still had the small, stubborn jaw, the pert little nose and the wide, warm, soft pink mouth. It occurred to me, suddenly, that it was distinctly kissable, that mouth. But it was a little too late for me to do anything about it, now.

"Will you take tarrojan, my dear? I believe you have already met my grand-daughter, Cn. Everest?" Madame Lyntonhurst asked sweetly.

"I have had that pleasure, yes ma'm," I replied gravely. "Some hours ago she blew out my brains with a hand-laser."

It wasn't much of a dig but Meade flinched a little. I didn't pursue it or try to improve upon it at that time. Not to spare the girl, of course. People who make a good try at frying my skull with a hand-laser have already forfeited their rights to Marquis of Queensberry treatment—at least in my book.

But I was thinking over the implications in that word "Granddaughter." *Grand*daughter indeed! Not very likely. *Great-great*-granddaughter would be more like it. But the curt pronunciation of the term, coming from Madame Lyntonhurst, was interesting. Revealing. The old woman still had a very feminine set of instincts . . . and just how old *was* she, anyway?

As you can see, I was hunting for a weapon. Any weapon. There are damn few ways a man tied down can fight back but a well-honed tongue, a clever brain and a canny set of wits make pretty fair weapons in a pinch.

But no time for this now. She was speaking to me. These thoughts had occupied only a tenth of a second and Madame Lyntonhurst was still reacting to my blunt gibe.

"Come, Citizen, no hard words, please! I asked you if you would have a cup, my dear. I am not accustomed to repeating myself."

Keeping her lashes lowered and her eyes fixed on the carpet, not looking at me, Meade said in a soft, subdued voice, "No thank you, grandmother."

"Then sit down, my dear. Citizen Everest and I were just getting acquainted. Sit there," she said, indicating a chair with a gesture of one beautifully-manicured hand. Meade said, "Yes, thank you, grandmother," in a low hesitant voice and sat down quickly, tucking the skirts of her long tunic modestly around her tanned bare knees.

She was a completely different person in the presence of her grandmother. Gone was the bold, bright, gutsy girl of before. This young woman was modest, shy, diffident and subdued. A prickling went over my scalp. I could understand what being raised by this sweet, saintly, patrician old lady might be like. I felt like vomiting. Poor Meade. . . .

The old woman looked at her with gentle eyes.

"I *do* wish you would join this young man and me, dear, in a cup of tarrojam. Really, it is an excellent brew."

Meade flushed slightly but her voice was still hushed and subdued and she kept her eyes down as she feebly protested, "Really, grandmother, I don't feel like. . . ."

"Actually, dear," her grandmother's sweetly reasonable tone over-rode her objections, "it is considered rather bad manners to refuse a cup . . . surely I have trained you in better habits of social etiquette than this. I really do think you should have a cup, darling. You look just a bit tired and pale."

"Very well, grandmother. I will have a cup, thank you." Meade's colorless voice was scarcely audible. Smiling sweetly, the old woman poured a third cup of the steaming beverage, inquired solicitously as to whether Meade would prefer nace or thoroway with her tarrojan and handed her cup over with a polite little interchange of "Thank you, grandmother," and "You are very welcome, dear." Something about this small display of petty cruelty I found sickening.

The room was immaculate, exquisitely appointed and redolent of fresh-cut flowers and fragrant cups of tarrojan but it housed a loathsome and disgusting abnormality, like a hidden and monstrous cancer, putrescent and infectuous.

But the old lady was speaking to me again.

"She's a remarkable young woman, don't you think, Cn. Everest? Intelligent, pretty in a way and very quick. I have trained her myself from the time she was just a little child. Don't you agree that she makes a singular intelligence agent?"

The question hung there on the air, waiting to be answered. I was gettting weary of all this pretense and eager to get down to the point. I also felt like disturbing that cool, queenly serenity.

So I pursed my lips judiciously and shook my head.

"No, actually I'd say she's remarkably stupid at it. I knew her for a phoney with the first word out of her mouth," I said in a level voice.

Meade flinched a little in her chair and raised her dark lustrous eyes to flick me with just the slightest glance. But Madame Lyntonhurst did not turn a hair.

"Really, young man? You sound quite precise. What, pray tell, gave her away to you so swiftly?" she inquired with the air of humoring me, as if I was being deliberately bad-tempered and affrontive.

"Citadel people, when they meet in a place where they might possibly be over-heard, use a very simple vocal code to identify themselves to each other," I said bluntly. "The first one to speak begins his first sentence with the word 'but,' to which the proper response of the other member of Citadel is to begin his or her sentence with the word 'indeed.' I used the code but your granddaughter did not. Hence, I assumed she was not from Citadel at all but was only pretending to be."

Madame Lyntonhurst smiled graciously.

"That hardly seems sufficient evidence on which

to found so important a suspicion, if I may say so," she murmured.

I laughed. "You don't understand. By the time they put me in with your darling grand-daughter, I was already fairly certain of what was going on. Meade's mistakes merely proved what I had already guessed."

That got to her, all right. A small tight vertical wrinkle appeared between her arched brows, where (obviously) no wrinkle would be tolerated.

"Continue, please," Madame Lyntonhurst said.

"The first tip-off was that your gunmen left me wearing my own clothes," I explained brusquely. "No outfit that big, that well equipped, that professional, could possibly permit a captive Citadel man to retain his own clothing. Popular legend accounts us as being clever people equipped with all sorts of cunning gadgetry. But your boys permitted me to wear my private arsenal—something only the dumbest amateurs would do."

"I see. . . ."

"Then the fat politician in command of the ship came down to have his med check me out. The med gave me the most cursory going-over in history and said I had only received a grazing blast from the stungun and was coming out of it. This was untrue, although I was faking pretty well. But the second tip-off was that he had an e.e.g. in his kit but didn't use it. Now, the logical way to check a man for unconsciousness is to slap an electrode on him and get a count of his brain activity. That would be something I couldn't fake—my brain was either consciously active or unconsciously dormant. The med didn't use the e.e.g. because he had been told not to. The fat politician—"

"Commissioner Kellering," the old woman supplied.

125

"Kellering, obviously had instructed his med in just what to do and just what conclusion to announce. I guessed that Kellering assumed, and quite rightly, that Citadel members are not caught napping quite so easily and he was planning on my permitting myself to be captured while pretending to be blotto. At the time they had some sort of electroencephalograph pinned on me from another cabin and announced via an audiobeam to Kellering exactly how awake I really was. I know this because I overheard part of the audiobeam report to Kellering. I didn't catch all of it because I wasn't listening for a transmission. As it was, all I caught was the 'peaks' of the wave, you might say. Sounded like code, or pure nonsense—all I heard was something that sounded like 'GEERPTSFOOMENELGTIVTEEEFF.' "

"Yet you made sense out of that gibberish, I assume?"

I nodded. "Sure. But not right away. Before long I figured out what it meant, by trying to fill in vowel sounds between those peaks, which were mostly, I noticed, hard consonants. It didn't take me long to realize the audiobeam report had been more or less to this effect: 'E.E.G. reports full mental activity, chief.' Cut out most of the vowels and run that all together and you get something that sounds rather like 'GEERPTSFOOMENELGTIVTEEEFF.' "

"And what did you deduce from this?"

I grinned. "It was becoming pretty obvious. They grabbed me but left me in possession of most of my gadgets because they wanted me to escape later on— why, I did not at once know. But, immediately after learning that I was wide awake and listening to everything, Fatboy Kellering said, loud and clear, that his thugs were to toss me in the brig with 'the other Citadel agent.' It was obvious by now that this was

126

said for my benefit. They wanted me to believe Meade was a Citadel agent. So in I went—the brig under a convenient dampener field so that I couldn't probe Meade mentally and get at the truth. *And also so I would not find out that Meade was a telepath—the same telepath who had tried to snoop me in Demaratus Station!"*

That got past the old dragon's guard, all right! She blinked and paled ever so little.

In aristocratic society, in this great Imperium of ours, a telepath is regarded as something not quite well-bred, as mental disease or venereal infections were frowned upon in the upper crust of earlier societies. I could see that Madame Lyntonhurst did not at all like the fact that I had stumbled onto Meade's T-powers. Telepaths were mighty useful to have around but not in the drawing room. I decided to rub it in a little, before moving on.

"In fact," I drawled, "I had been wrong about your agent, Dom, the little fat man who led the first ambush party against me. I assumed he was the snooper. But it had been Meade all the time. She spotted my mindlock—an ordinary spaceman like me had no good reason to be wearing so expensive a mindlock, only Naval officers, Crown couriers, heralds, important businessmen, *crooks and intelligence agents* wear mindlocks. She tipped off Dom. He rode down in the shuttle with me and followed me to the headquarters of the Rim Star Association, which clinched the guess that I might be the Citadel agent sent to investigate the disturbance in the fringes of the galactic magnetic field; and he set up the ambush.

"When he shot me down with the stungun, I remembered having seen him in the shuttle, and just automatically assumed he was the one who tried to snoop me up in the terminal. But later on, when I

127

was battling to control his mind, I should have noticed he had *dormant* T-centers. At the time, I was too busy fighting for this to register. It didn't hit me until later.

"Yep, it was later on that I realized it was your dear, precious, darling granddaughter, and not poor old Dom, who was the . . . *freak*."

A long time ago, when the first terran telepaths were discovered and started being trained, an ignorant, hostile and intolerant citizenry had selected that term to use on people with T-powers. "Freak" became one of those automatically dirty words with which mankind sneered at anyone not quite the same as itself. A word in the same class with Nigger, Sheeny, Spic, Wop, Papist, Commie, and all the rest.

It sometimes takes generations—even centuries—for one of these unlovely labels to lose its bite. I was gambling on the fact that Grandma was an old, old lady, and a patrician, since it is the prideful aristocrat who retains intolerance the longest. And I was right. She knew what *freak* meant, all right.

For the first time since our little *tête-à-tête* began, Madame Lyntonhurst lost her graciousness and elegance and poise. It did my heart good to see that sweet old-lady mouth take on an ugly twist—to watch the warmth go out of her eyes—to see them go as cold and hard, as dull and opaque as cut agate.

"You have a loose tongue in you for a young man who will be dead meat before morning," she said harshly.

THIRTEEN

"Maybe, but we were calling a spade a spade, weren't we, ma'm?" I grinned.

I had to hand it to her, she recovered her control fast.

"Continue, young man. But without the—" she shot a veiled glance at Meade, sitting bowed over in her chair "—*obscenities*, if you please."

Meade flinched as the remark hit home. It was a conditioned reflex, that flinch, not a raw wound. And right then I knew the hook the old lady had used to control the girl. All her young life her grandmother had used the girl's telepathic gifts, like some sort of deformity, to twist her around one of those slender, elegant, patrician fingers. And I hated the old woman right then as much as I have ever hated in all my centuries.

I was also thinking as hard and fast and furiously as I have had to think in millennia. I was in one Plenum of a tough spot and the only way I could get out of it was to get that dampener switched off. None of these people had the slightest conception of just how powerful my mind really was. They assumed I was an ordinary telepath, maybe a bit more than ordinary, say—class 12, at a guess. If they could have watched me battling for control of Dom they might have gained some conception of just what I can do. But I had good reason to believe that battle had gone un-observed, although they knew how it came out, of course—with me on top. But any combination of accident and circumstance could account for that.

And my feat of making Meade think she had brained me with the hand-laser during our abortive getaway from the freighter—that was something any telepath could do if he had stronger T-powers than the telepath he was controlling (and I estimated Meade at a class 10 level, no more than that, surely).

I was, at this time, so far as I knew, the only Star class mind the race had ever produced. And no one alive but myself knew this.

So Madame L had no particular reason to be afraid of me or to take any but the ordinary, sensible precautions dictated by reason and experience. After all, she had telepaths of her own—her darling granddaughter was surely not the only T-mind in this conspiracy. Psychologically, my position was clear. She was the Queen Bee of her little private imperium and I was the lonely, friendless, no-ace-up-the-sleeve stranger. This was her own hive—why should she be afraid of helpless little me?

Now standard procedures suggested, with all the force of tradition, that I should keep my mouth shut and avoid giving the old lady any information at all.

But these were very special circumstances and I had to improvise as I went along. This is why I was blabbing away, pouring out info and giving precise, documented criteria as to why I had suspected the whole phoney thing from the beginning. I wanted to convince the old hag that the deleo settings I had blurted out to Meade back in the gig were the prime "phonus balonus"—which they were. And the quicker I made her believe this, the quicker she would put me under interrogation—with drugs, I hoped. Drugs I could handle because of my ability to control my own physiological machinery to an extent unsuspected by the Opposition.

And with poor me squirted full of babble-juice and

tongue-loosener, why should they keep the dampener turned on?

Answer: they wouldn't.

"So," I continued rubbing it in, "after your darling granddaughter flubbed the recognition code test, I let her convict herself with her own mouth—which she did repeatedly with the first two dozen words she spoke to me."

Madame Lyntonhurst arched one brow incredulously.

I laughed. "Well . . . look. Once upon a time there was a place called 'San Francisco.'" I added, reading her blank expression, "Oh, this is ancient history. On Sol III, before the First Imperium, before the Nordonnate or even the United Systems, in fact, San Francisco was a city in a place called California. Well, to everybody else in the country, for some odd reason, San Francisco was known familiarly as 'Frisco.' Plenum knows who coined this nickname, or when, or why—"

"I presume this lecture on antiquarian folkways has relevance to our conversation?"

"Yes ma'm, you presume correctly. Anyway, for some even odder reason, the San Franciscans themselves regarded this slangy, if not barbaric appellation, with extreme distaste. The diminutive was, in their eyes, or to their ears, not an affectionate one. They got quite cranky on the subject of 'Frisco.' I mean, you could get a bloody nose that way."

I did not mention that this had actually happened to me, once upon a time—for obvious reasons.

"Same thing happened later in the same century, when Luna, the satellite of Sol III, was settled. The colonists were indignant to the point of being ferocious about being called 'Loonies.' And not at all for the obvious reason that in English (the dominant

131

language of the period) the term had the slang connotation of insanity. No, Siree, the colonists referred to *themselves* as 'Lunatics'—a term with the *same* connotation."

"Antiquarian folkways, and now a lesson in extinct languages," my hostess murmured.

"Well, the point I'm laying the groundwork for, is just this: it is odd but true that members of Citadel refer to Citadel as Citadel. That's all—Citadel."

"I fail to see—"

"Your girl here called it '*the* Citadel' three times running, in the first two minutes of our first conversation," I said.

A silence ensued.

"Something no Citadel member would *ever* do. Oh, maybe once, absent-mindedly. But she repeated the term three times in as many sentences."

Madame Lyntonhurst regarded me fixedly and without expression.

"I see," she said at last.

"Oh, she caught on fast enough," I added, for some reason. "She's got a brain in that pretty head. She heard me call the organization 'Citadel' a couple of times, and adapted her speech accordingly from then on. But three times was too incredible a slip for a bona fide Citadel member to make."

"Was there anything else?"

"Sure. I led her on a bit. The first thing you knew she was calling Citadel 'members' Citadel 'agents' and she asked me if I had been assigned to the same 'case' as the one she was on Demaratus to investigate. Citadel members are assigned to *projects*, not 'cases.' "

"I see your point, young man. Of course Meade could not have foreknowledge of specific organizational slang and it is true that any organization that

132

survives long enough evolves a private language out of its own traditions."

"You said it, lady. You should hear the sort of technicalese the boys in the drive room bandy among themselves. You gotta be an engineer to understand engineers. Anyway, after these bloopers, I led her on just a bit, to sort of clinch the matter. I told her not to worry, once she failed to make her twice-a-day report to Base the Grand Admiral would know somebody had grabbed her—or words to that general effect."

"What was wrong with that?" Meade asked. It was the first time she had spoken to me since she entered the room. Her eyes were big and solemn and troubled. I felt a small inward lift in the morale department. I don't know quite why, but it was a small victory somehow.

"Members of Citadel assigned to a project don't make reports twice a day, and don't call them 'twice-a-days.' And the commanding officer of Citadel is not a Grand Admiral, he's an Acting Colonel. Plus the fact that Citadel headquarters is called *Headquarters*, not 'Base.' I knew you were a spy planted on me before I was in your company five minutes," I said. And I said it straight to her in a level, noncommittal voice.

Of course I didn't tell Meade the other big mistake she had made during our initial conversation. It was maybe the biggest blooper of them all. I mean, when I told her my name was Saul Everest. She didn't so much as blink an eye—and that was wrong. Very, very wrong.

I am something of a legend to Citadel members (I ought to be, since I am the original Founding Father of the whole shebang), and had Meade been a legiti-

mate member of the secret organization she would
have jumped about a foot in the air when I announced
who I was.

But this extra scrap of evidence I naturally kept to
myself. I could hardly wish to have my unique status
as an immortal known to members of the Opposition.

These points hammered home, I turned from the
blank-faced girl and devoted my attentions to Madame Lyntonhurst again. All the evidence was out in
the open now—time to sum things up. "So now I
knew why I had been left with my built-in arsenal
intact. They wanted me to buy the fact that Meade
was a Citadel member like myself and Meade was all
primed with a super-urgent message that just had to
get back to Citadel—this being the motive for me to
try an escape. If I hadn't had a magnetic field projector stashed in my boot, they presumed I had a
couple other tricks I could pull, like anesthetic needles
or miniature gas bombs or hypnotic rings or something. If worse came to worse, I suppose they were
willing to let an apparently careless guard turn his
back on me so I would knock him silly and use his
gun to burn my way out," I said, carefully watching
her eyes.

"Then, when we were making our escape, your
bully boys were all prepared to knock me cockeyed
with a carefully-aimed anti-personnel field which
would not hit Meade because she was to make a big
scene over struggling into her airsuit in free fall—
not touching any metal—'grounded.' Then, with me
groggy, almost ready to conk out, arms and legs
paralyzed, the freighter turning about to catch us in
their scopes, only seconds from death or recapture,
Meade was to tearfully pry out of me the deleo
settings used to make an emergency call to Citadel
Headquarters.

"And *that* was what this whole elaborate production was all about," I concluded.

The defense rests, I thought to myself.

Madame Lyntonhurst examined her perfectly manicured nails during the ensuing silence. Then:

"Come here to me, my dear," she said softly.

"Grandmother, please!"

"Come here."

The girl got up and went over to the big chair where her grandmother was sitting.

"A little closer, Meade. And bend down your head just a bit. Don't make Grandmother have to *reach*, dear."

Soft, gentle words and a sweetly smiling face. Then why was the base of my spine cold and crawling?

Meade bent slowly, her face averted from me. Madame Lyntonhurst reached up and cupped the girl's chin in her hand.

"You have been a wicked, naughty girl. And you have been a disappointment to your Grandmother. Aren't you sorry for what you have done, dear? Tell Grandmother how sorry you feel," she said. The room was deathly quiet. I wished I didn't have to watch what I knew was coming but somehow I couldn't turn my gaze aside. There is something fascinating about sickness. . . .

"I am *very* sorry I have been so bad, Grandmother," Meade said in a faint voice, stiffly, her lips pinched in the grip of those long slim pale aristocratic fingers.

"But you are aware that merely feeling sorry is not enough, isn't that true, dear?" the old woman asked. The horrible thing about it was the sweetly *reasonable* tone of her voice.

"Yes, Grandmother," Meade whispered in a voice almost inaudible.

135

"Then you agree that you should be punished for your mistakes, isn't that true, dear?"

"Y-yes."

"In fact, you *want* to be punished. That is true, is it not?"

"Yes," very faintly.

"Then ask Grandmother for the favor."

I felt like vomiting. Like yelling, like breaking things. But somehow I could not interrupt this obscene thing that stretched between the old woman and the young girl. And, somehow, I knew they were alone. In a private universe. I could not intrude on what they were doing, no matter how much I hungered to.

"Please, Grandmother."

"Please *what*, darling?"

"Please punish me, Grandmother!"

"Grandmother *dear*," the old woman said in gentle reproof.

"Please punish me, Grandmother dear." Mechanically.

"Very well, my dear, if you are quite certain that this is what *you* want. . . ."

I watched, fascinated, as she sank her fingernails into the girl's face.

They were polished and buffed, the nails on that old and regal hand. They were long and sharp and pointed. They pressed slowly into the tender young flesh, made red crescents and cut in deeper.

The thumb was set above Meade's mouth. Its nail sank slowly into her upper lip. Strong. Cruel. I *saw* the pressure, the tendon stretch, rising to stand out from the withered skin.

The other nails were set in the cheek and in the soft flesh just under the chin. They sank in slowly.

Meade made a muffled whimper, a baby sound.

136

But she did not move or draw away from the hand and what it was doing to her face.

The Kyrian stardrop glittered on that hand.

I watched a trickle of scarlet dribble down upon the white fingers, and smear the fabulous gem.

Madame Lyntonhurst made a sound of disgust and annoyance. She released the girl's face and fastidiously wiped the red smear from hand and ring on a snowy napkin. She did not look at me.

"That's all, my dear," she said in a matter-of-fact tone. "Go wash your face now and get ready for bed. You should have retired *hours* ago."

Meade straightened up slowly. She took her own napkin, pressed it over her leaking face and went docilely from the room. She closed the door gently behind her and we were left alone, the old woman and I.

Madame Lyntonhurst touched the side of the pot.

"Dear me, our tarrojan has grown cool. I'll put the pot back on the heatplate and we'll have another cup while we finish our little chat, young man," she said calmly.

"Won't that be nice!" I remarked. But she did not deign to answer.

FOURTEEN

"Of course, there really is no Intruder," I observed a moment later. "No mysterious invader from the Magellanics. No wandering star scouting the Rim—dark or otherwise."

She poured a fresh cup of the fragrant beverage.

"Are you certain of that?"

"Quite certain, ma'm. It was all part of this huge, elaborate scheme to flush a Citadel investigator out of the underbrush. I don't quite know how it was worked, the magnetic disturbance I mean, but I can make a guess."

"Pray do. I believe you said thoroway . . ."

"Yes. Probably with a ship. A big one—large enough to mount grav projectors on a new scale of immensity. The ship probably was made the center of an artificial gravity field thousands, even tens of thousands of times stronger than anything ever attempted before. Such a gravity field would certainly warp the magnetic lines of force around the fringes of the galaxy, just as the gravitational field of a Red Dwarf warps them in nature."

"Quite a good guess. Upwards of two million g is the actual figure," she commented.

She set my cup down on the edge of the table nearest to me, where I could easily reach it. But there was no chance of my making a grab for her wrist. The tangle-field restraining the motion of my legs denied me the leverage I needed to make the lunge. And, since I had to drag against the surface tension of the field, my timing would be off and any

139

lunge I tried would have to be a ludicrous slow-motion thing which she could easily avoid. So no lunging.

"I can even make a not-so-wild guess as to why you wanted to spot a Citadel man at all," I remarked.

"Pray do," she said sweetly.

"Citadel is a myth, a legend of the spaceways. Its occasional interventions in history have been as unobtrusive as possible. Whenever Citadel has had to assassinate or otherwise remove an Imperator or hegemon or Centumvir from office, it was made to seem completely natural. Not the slightest shred of historical documentation has ever been permitted to exist which could prove that Citadel is anything more than a rumor . . . a legend of remote, implacable, omniscient mystery-mahatmas subtly influencing the direction of history for their unguessable and inscrutable ends. *And before you make your try at taking over the government, you want to find out whether Citadel really does exist,*" I said casually, dropping my bombshell into the suddenly still room.

She said nothing, merely watched me with a polite non-committal smile.

"After all, even a conspiracy as big as the one you're running can't afford to risk the chance that Citadel might not be just a fairy-tale," I continued. "Hence this torturous scheme to net one of us and secure some basic information. Because if Citadel *is* real, you've got to consider it as a major factor in any take-over. And if it *is* real, then maybe you can infiltrate it, or subvert it, or buy it. Or destroy it."

" 'Take over the government' . . . isn't that a rather grandiose concept?" she murmured. "Certainly a melodramatic one. . . ."

"Oh, it's not so farfetched as all that," I replied.

140

"Kermian has ruled for twenty-seven years now and he succeeded to the Dais as an old man. His health has never been robust. Next year, or in a year or two or three, he will die. And the Heir of Tregephon, the only son of his younger brother, now deceased, is only a child. There will have to be a Regency, the third such in Imperial history. And I have a hunch you have somebody already picked out for the job! Somebody who is so deeply in your debt, or so much under your thumb, that the effective balance of power tips right into your lap. How's that for a wild guess, eh?"

She made no comment.

"And after you've gained control of the Lord Regent, what happens? Does the young Heir die after a few years, as soon as you have consolidated your position—die, after naming the Regent as his successor? Or does the Heir survive to assume the Dais? But by then you will have corrupted or broken him —just as your granddaughter has been broken and crushed? Either way, I must congratulate you. The plan is virtually fool-proof."

And then it came. I had been waiting for it.

"You are quite a clever young man," Madame Lyntonhurst said slowly. "You have an ability I greatly admire . . . the rare power to piece together isolated hints and bits of data into an integrated whole. The Party can use young people like yourself."

I couldn't help laughing. I had to set my cup down before I spilled tarrojan all over those gorgeous carpets.

"Is my offer so amusing, young man?" Just the hint of chill reproof in those gracious, cultured tones.

"I laugh to keep from vomiting," I said levelly.

141

"Lady, I wouldn't work for you for all the units in the Imperial mint. I step on snakes; I don't work for them!"

She did not deign to make an answer to this. Instead, she raised her voice a trifle and spoke to empty air.

"Control, you may let him enter now."

One wall opened up and a—*thing*—came through.

It sat in a hover-chair. It had to, for what I could see of its legs under the thermal were twisted and deformed.

I say "it" because I could not tell whether the thing was male or female. There wasn't much in the way of a face, just a bloated hairless skull, enormously swollen. The rest of the face was scar-tissue. And there was one eye. That eye fixed on me a cold, intense scrutiny. I have never seen such concentrated essence of hatred in a look.

"This is the man," Madame Lyntonhurst said, indicating me.

And then the dampener field went off and my mind was free.

The next moment I got the shock of my life.

I was under the attack of a mind every bit as powerful as my own.

A probe of tremendous resiliency and power struck my shields a terrific blow. I had raised them instinctively, the microsecond that the dampener ceased exerting its restraint on my T-powers. Never had I felt a probe of such impact. It was all I could do to repel it and strike a blow with a probe of my own. I met a shield of enormous density—many times stronger than any shield I had ever encountered.

And then I was fighting for my very life. . . .

This creature was no immortal like myself. Yet it

142

had a Star-class mind and T-powers at least as powerful as my own, perhaps even a bit stronger. But I knew it could not be an immortal, not with deformities so extensive as to require a chair life support system—for I could see the tubes connecting its circulatory and urinogenital systems with concealed mechanisms in the chair. No, it was mortal enough, but a genetic freak—perhaps a genuine mutation on the basic hominid stock. Nature had used a cruel sort of justice in this case, balancing a horribly warped and useless body with a mind of incredible power and brilliance.

I had occasionally wondered what it would be like to be pitted against a telepath with a Star-class mind as strong as my own. I had thought that I was the only Star the terran race had ever produced. Now I discovered my error. There *was* another Star-class mind in the galaxy . . . but a mind twisted and poisoned with hatred and envy . . . bent awry and corrupted into the service of the powers of greed and unscrupulous ambition.

If Madame Lyntonhurst had an ally like this in her pay, then I had been woefully negligent in underestimating the calibre and resources of her organization. With a Star-class telepath in its ranks, this conspiracy had chances for success enormously superior to anything I had imagined.

As suddenly and as unexpectedly as the mental duel had begun—it ended.

The remorseless attack ceased. The crushing pressure faded. The dampener field snapped on again and I was left gasping in my chair, shaken by the virulence and the intensity of the assault. But the attacker had not breached my defenses. The twisted, faceless thing in the hover-chair had not penetrated my

143

mind, draining it of information. But the assault had given it knowledge of just how powerful a telepath I was. . . .

The creature in the chair tittered in a vile, gloating way.

"Strong . . . strong!" it rasped. "Stronger than I had guessed . . . there is a mystery about this man . . . something hidden and vital . . . but I will have his secrets, all his secrets . . . soon, soon!" It had a nasty cackling laugh that sent chills up my spine.

Madame Lyntonhurst asked calmly, "Do you anticipate any difficulty in probing his mind? Will it take much time? We must have the answers to certain questions as soon as possible."

The deformed thing flopped about in its chair glaring at me with a cunning, leering eye.

"I will be a battle of two powerful minds," the thing grated harshly. "But I can break his mind. It will not take long.

"Control, you may remove our guest to his quarters now," she said to the unseen watchers. And—just like that—the long, exhausting interview was over.

They took me down the hall towards my cell. A dampener was on me all the way, the guards were armed with stunners and neuronic goads and my legs were under mild restraint and my arms secured, so there was not the slightest chance of making a break for freedom.

All the way to the cell my mind kept running over and over one track. One word.

Suicide.

With the information in my head, Madame Lyntonhurst could infiltrate Headquarters with ease. I knew all the codes, the recognition signals, the secret bases, the organizational set-up. I knew the location of Headquarters and how to approach it and gain entry. I knew everything there was to know about the defensive systems and how to circumvent them. If a good deep probe ever read me, why, armed with what I knew about Citadel, Madame Lyntonhurst could just about land an invasion fleet on Headquarters.

And there was just no way of estimating what she could do, once Citadel was under her control. The secret organization had members and observers at every power center, in every ministry, at every level of power in the government of the Imperium. Then again, Citadel had built up an exclusive arsenal of advanced technology over the ages. Weapons that could kill without leaving a trace. Weapons that could conquer—or decimate—half a galaxy.

In her unscrupulous hands, Citadel would become the most terrible weapon ever conceived.

And I knew that I alone could keep Citadel from her grasp. No one else could do this job for me.

Or *could* I? Helpless, alone, ringed in with enemies, held incommunicado in the very stronghold of the Opposition, my T-powers negated, pitted against all the strength and vicious cunning of a mind as powerful as any in human history—how could I hope to keep back the information they were after?

It would not be a matched duel of equal minds, I knew grimly. Surely they would attempt to leach and exhaust my conscious control, to crush my will, before permitting that cruel tittering thing in the chair to probe the ruins of my mind.

It would be easy. All they had to do was shoot my blood-stream full of scopolamine-*gamma* and my will would be subjugated and enthralled. Or unhinge my consciousness with an overdose of lysergic acid diethylamide . . . with enough LSD churning through my system, I wouldn't even know I was *being* probed.

145

No, there was only one way out. Never before had I ever really contemplated it in all seriousness but now it was the only means I could use to ensure that the vital information in my mind could not be used against civilization but would die with me.

Suicide!

It would be very easy. My control over the involuntary functions of my body was such that I could probably kill myself within a few seconds. Even with my T-centers blanked out by the dampener, I could cause hemorrhage or heart failure. With luck I could kill myself swiftly enough so that they could not repair the damage in time to salvage my memory. The brain dies slowly, I knew. The mind, that intangible web of neural connections, takes longer to perish than the engine of flesh that sustains and houses it. But perhaps I could do it without discovery—say, while pretending to go to sleep.

I should have realized that they would outguess me on this.

Midway to the cell I pitched forward into the arms of the guards—shot from behind with a stungun.

And after that . . . just blackness.

FIFTEEN

For days now I had been crossing the bone-dry desert on foot and now I was very near the end of my endurance.

Like the flaming eyes of some mad god, the twin suns of Selidar blazed down from a cloudless sky.

The powdery, ochre sands crunched under my bootheels. Dry and hot were those sands. Waves of heat rose shimmering from them. The air was like the breath of a baking-oven.

My eyelids were swollen half-shut. I could see very little. Everything swam in a dim haze of crimson. There was no sound, no sound at all, save for the harsh sobbing as I strove to breathe in that dry scorching air.

It was two days now since I had drained the last drop from the container and flung its useless weight from me with a hoarse, despairing curse. Two days in this furnace-glare of perpetual noon without water.

My lips were cracked and puffy. My tongue was black and swollen—swollen so large that I could no longer close my mouth. My muscles were stiff and lame. My feet were sore and bleeding and blistered in the torturous ovens of my boots. My Japon had torn to rags in a struggle with a cannibal vine days ago. By now my chest and back and shoulders were raw and horrible with second-degree burns. The rest of my body was as dry and desiccated as old leather. The glaring, motionless suns had sucked every drop of moisture from my flesh and left it burnt black.

147

I staggered up the slope of another dune, wading through drifts of the loose powdery sand, and reached the crest . . . to see yet another dune ahead of me. And another. And another. And another. . . .

How many dunes had I crossed in the burning days and nights of this endless inferno? Hundreds? Thousands? And how many more must I conquer before I sink exhausted into the searing and smothering embrace of the parched sands . . . and leave my bones, crisp forever in the furnace of this devil-world of eternal noon?

I began to tremble from exhaustion. My knees folded and I sank to all fours like some worn and weary beast on the dune crest. Spasms of self-pity shook my body. I sobbed, great hoarse hacking sobs of defeat and hopelessness.

But I could not weep. There was no longer enough moisture in my flesh to make a single tear. . . .

The glare of the nebula, reflected from the cracked mirrors of the ice, blinded me.

It burned through my half-shut eyes, thrusting needles of exquisite agony deep into my brain.

I longed to rest here for awhile, to gather my strength, but I knew that to cease moving was to start dying. For the rips in my thermal suit were leaking warmth faster than the suit could replace it. I could no longer feel my feet. They were dead, numb lumps of insensitive matter.

How long ago had it been since my skimmer had cracked up in the swirling snow storm? How long now had the hunched, white-furred predators hunted me across the endless icefields? Weeks . . . or only days? I could no longer remember. I crouched there, resting against the numb cushion of the soft snow, feeling the weariness in my body bone deep.

Above me the colossal shining glory of the nebula filled the cold black sky with intolerable splendor.

It was like some vast, soundless explosion caught and fixed forever changeless in a split-second exposure. Intolerably beautiful and intolerably brilliant, that titanic flowering cloud of cold green fire that blossomed across two thirds of the sky. *Oh, if only I could rest. . . .*

The muffled baying of remorseless hounds awoke me.

The hunting things still tracked me through the glittering wastes of this frozen world. And they were near—near!

Danger sent adrenalin pumping through me. A surge of strength jolted me to my feet. I had sunk deep into the smothering blanket of soft thick snow. Now as I floundered free I discovered that my dead frozen feet would not support me. The slow heat-leakage had numbed my legs to the thigh. I staggered and fell down, and lay gasping and sobbing.

Again that eerie wail from the frozen plains behind me. The heavy, tireless predators were almost upon me . . . I *must* get up . . . must somehow find the strength to flee from them. Like obscene and cowardly jackals, they feared to attack me while I moved and lived. But what if I could not move, could not even rise? Would they ring me in—cold green eyes burning with the same icy fires as that vast frozen cloud of glory that filled the wintry skies— and pull me down with those horrible jaws, tearing through my thermal suit to rip out my throat, fierce fangs crunching through my flesh, drinking my hot blood?

Somehow I fought my way to my knees. They would support me, even though I could not feel them. But further than this I could not rise. I did

149

not have the strength. And the cold, the black wither-
ing bitter cold, seeping through the rents in my suit,
numbing my flesh . . . draining my small store of
strength. . . .

Then I saw them. Hunched, heavy-shouldered
things with mean cold eyes wherein blazed a mania-
cal hunger. Snarling black muzzles lifting to reveal
sharp cruel fangs. Lean, powerful bodies all sinewy
rippling strength under thick white fur. Ugly brutes
they were, an uncanny mingling of panther and wolf,
and terrible engines of ferocity and fighting strength,
for all their cowardice.

And the Barringer at my hip was useless, its energy
cell exhausted hours or days or eternities ago.

Hunched on my knees, dead legs helpless under me,
I watched them gather and circle in for the kill. . . .

All I could think of was water. *Water:* cold, fresh,
sparkling, pure. My thirst was like some devouring
cancer, slowly spreading its fiery tendrils of pain
through every nerve, every cell, every muscle, organ
and tissue of my exhausted, desiccated body. . . .

The irony was that I was surrounded with water, all
around me, everywhere, as far as the eye could see.
Sliding wet glistening surfaces of limpid cool blue
crystal water.

> *Water, water everywhere*
> *And not a drop to drink.*

The sky was a cloudless huge dome of hot acety-
lene blue and it burned like a sheet of flame. I had used
the rags of my tunic to make a rude shelter against the
blistering sun but even the shade was sweltering.

It was a week or more since the hovercar had ruptured a spanson, skewed about, lost the "plane" of
the sea's surface, and sunk like a stone.

150

And it was three days . . . three dry, roasting days of torture . . . since I had licked up the last lukewarm drop of fresh water in the container.

The heat and thirst were killing me, I knew. Drop by drop the searing blue flame of the sky sucked the moisture out of my body. Another day . . . perhaps another hour . . . and I would go mad.

At first, while my water supply still lasted, I had relieved the fiery torments of the sun by sliding over the edge of the sponge-plastic raft and immersing my almost naked body up to the throat in the cool blue water. But no more. Now I endured the torture and waited for death. I did not dare tempt myself by lowering my weary sunburnt flesh into the chill wet embrace of the gliding sea.

With the sparkling waves only inches below my lips, I knew I could not for long control the longing to drink. Sooner or later I would weaken and duck my head and fill my throat with the horrible, burning stickiness of salt water.

Long ago, marooned on the planet-wide seas of Vanadis, I had watched a Citadel comrade die raving in convulsions from drinking seawater. And while I retained a grasp on my sanity, I would not go that road myself.

Strangely enough, I was no longer hungry. Two or three days ago, when I exhausted the last crumb of my emergency rations, it had been hunger that tormented me. Thoughts of food had filled every waking moment of the interminable hours. Torn by racking spasms of sheer hunger, I had chewed on the rags of my tunic, gnawed even on my fingers.

I had revolved a thousand feverish plans through my mind: fishing with a long thread unravelled from my tunic and a hook fashioned from a bent shoe fastener or playing dead until a sea bird settled on my supposed corpse to peck out my eyes, and strangling it and devouring it raw. Mad, wild schemes like these had seethed through my sun-baked brain during the long somnolent hours of day and the fitfull, nightmare-torn hours of night.

But there were no birds and there were no fish. Only the swaying mocking waves, the hot blue sky, the narrow raft and me.

Now I hungered no longer. The lust for food had dimmed and faded from my mind, withdrawing by gradual indeterminate stages until it was only a memory of pain, like an old lost love whose fires have died to cold ash.

Nothing was left but thirst.

I was in agony from thirst night and day. My dreams were wild jumbled visions of dewy fruits, sparkling forest pools, tall frosted goblets, cold lashing rains.

Once I awoke suddenly to find that I had dragged myself to the edge of the bobbing raft in my sleep and had dipped both hands into the sea. I sprang awake just as I was lifting my cupped hands to my parted lips. The shock, the horror of what I had almost done thrilled through me. For one unbelieving moment I stared down yearningly, like Tantalus, at the cold wetness trickling through my fingers. Then with a shudder of self-disgust I flung the water from me. But I rubbed my wet hands over the dry shrunken skin of my face. . . .

There were voices. From a great distance, dim and half-heard. I drifted on the surface of my dreams, listening absently to them but not really understanding or caring what they were saying.

A woman's voice, cold and reproving, "Even with the drug you haven't managed to break down his resistance yet. Time is growing short. You said it would be easy!"

Another voice, answering with a whining, peevish rasp, "He is strong . . . stronger than I would have dreamed! His defensive mechanism is unconscious and instinctive. It will take time . . ."

"We cannot spare the time. Have you learned nothing at all? Why can't you probe him? Surely his conscious mind is asleep."

"It is turned off, yes, but the part of the mind that never sleeps is aware of my intrusion and resists it, drawing upon some source of strength that seems inexhaustible. But I have learned a little from surface thoughts. You wanted to know what 'Citadel' means, why they chose that particular noun as the name of the organization. It seems to have no particular meaning but was chosen at random. If anything, it refers to the organization as a fortress standing sentinel, guarding liberty . . . an unconquerable stronghold."

"Anything else? You have been working on him for over an hour now."

"A few hints and guesses. His name is not Saul Everest. I attempted a probe of his identity center but his shield went up by instinctive reflex and I only got a glimpse."

"Everest is not his name then?"

"No, or rather . . . it is rather confused . . . it is only *one* of his names . . . perhaps the one he was born with, perhaps just a personal favorite among his pseudonyms. Oh, and something else. Although he is, or has until recently been, a Citadel agent and still identifies with the organization, I sense that he is on some sort of detached duty or extended leave, and not an active agent any longer."

The arguing voices went away for a little while as I dipped below the surface of sleep. Then, after a time, they swam back into focus and I listened to them passively, not really paying any attention to what the words meant, just registering them.

". . . No, not neoscopalomine derivatives, he has been already immunized to every varient in the pharmacopeia. I have been using a chemical derived from the ergot fungus group," said the rasping, querulous voice.

Then the first voice, the woman's voice, came again, "What does it do?"

"Chemically, it works in the bloodstream to block the body's manufacturing of 5-hydroxytryptamine. 5HT, we call it. When the 5HT levels in the brain are altered, bizarre aberrational effects similar to those experienced by habitual users of hallucinogens are caused. In other words, he experiences horribly real nightmares. I am using a shallow surface probe to suggest the current of his hallucinations. In effect, I am manipulating his subjective reality, trying to break down his protective reflexes through induced exhaustion and despair. He thinks he has been tortured with hunger, thirst, heat and cold for weeks."

"Can you get faster results through stronger dosages? Just so that he lives long enough to tell us what we want to know, after that he will be disposed of."

"The amount of the dose really isn't that significant. Once the 5HT level is altered the nightmarishly real hallucinations cannot be made *more* real."

"But what would a really massive dose do? Kill him?"

"No. Repeated use of the chemical inflicts a certain degree of damage to the chromosomes, that is all. But a truly massive dose might drive him over the edge into protective insanity. You know, of course, Madame, that insanity is basically the mind's last resort against a completely intolerable problem or situation.

154

Any one of the several illusory subrealities I have subjected him to would drive him insane if carried on long enough. I have been careful to switch to a new situation just before any given problem reaches the tolerance threshold."

"I should think that to drive him over the edge of madness would be the answer to our present dilemma. How can the mind of a catatonic, for example, resist the probe of an experienced telepath?" The suggestion was made in cool, clinical tones.

There was a shudder in the rasping voice as it answered this. "You would not think so, Madame, if you were a telepath. No one with T-powers would dare try to probe a mind driven totally insane. There is the danger of . . . infection."

Then the voices died away again and I slept . . . to wake in a living hell.

The stars laughed at me. They hated me that I was not a cold burning brilliance such as they but a floundering helpless thing of flesh and blood, lost and drifting in their immensities.

The recirculator wheezed in my ears, blowing its perpetual breath against my cheek. The radiometer squeaked and chattered, counting gamma particles as they flashed through me. The helmet light glowed dimly, just above my brow. My breath frosted the faceplate with a temporary blur of mist.

Stars hung above me, to either side, to the front and rear and below my dangling feet. They ringed me in. I floated at the center of a hollow sphere of stars.

Or did I float? Was I falling—falling—down . . . down . . . ever down . . . through eternity to the black and starless bottom of the universe? For an instant vertigo seized me in its giddy grip and I yelled like a mindless animal, loud, deafeningly loud, in the confines of my helmet. Was I falling forever through the black and empty gulfs between the stars—

> —*Him the almighty Power*
> *Hurl'd headlong flaming from th' ethereal sky,*
> *With hideous ruin and Combustion, down*
> *To bottomless perdition, there to dwell*
> *In adamantine chains and penal fire,*
> *Who durst defy th' Omnipotent to arms.*
> *Nine times the space that measures day and night*
> *To mortal men . . .*

The cold glitter of the mocking stars are unsleeping and sardonic eyes that stare and stare at me, as I flop and float and flounder here, tossed on the black and bitter winds that howl and sweep and blow forever in the gulfs between the worlds.

Nine times the space that measures day and night/ To mortal men . . . but men have lived nine days and nights in an airsuit before this, without going crazy. What is there to drive me crazy, just because I am lost and lonely, drifting between the stars in an airsuit that will be my bifurcated, air conditioned, centrally heated coffin until the great clock of entropy runs down and the universe collapses upon itself to expire, like Herodotus' phoenix, on the blazing pyre that is the fiery womb of its rebirth. My God! I am going mad! Think! Remember! Use your mind! Floating like this, no gravity, no feeling, is like those old-time experiments in sensory deprivation back before the Sino-Soviet holocaust touched off the Twenty-Nine Minute War in which America, my lost and loved America, died. They would put a man in a rubber suit with scuba gear, immerse him in lukewarm water with his arms and legs spread apart so that he couldn't touch himself. They would stop his ears, prop his

156

mouth open, blind his eyes, anesthetize all his sensations . . . and let him float until his mind went off in Cloud-Cuckoo-Land—just like I am now—ever since that CT micrometeorite went through my screens and hit the power center. Christ! If it hadn't been for the automatic ejection system that blew me clear I'd have gone up when the fusion core went up in one eye-searing fireball. Maybe it would have been best, that way—fast and clean, converted to a puff of protons before my nerve-endings even had time to send the first pain-impulse to my brain! Better than this living hell . . . *O my God that I haven't prayed to since I was a little child . . . O my sweet Christ in whose everlasting and infinite mercy I could never quite believe . . . O Jesus help me, Jesus, Jesus, Jesus. . . .*

The stink of my body almost suffocating me. Plenum, how close we are to the animal inside us, to the beast we really are but pretend we are not. Nine days in an airsuit and a civilized man stinks like an open sewer or an animal's cage in the zoo. Food and water to last for weeks, if you call reprocessed human piss *water* and concentrates *food*. By the Vuudh, what I wouldn't give for an honest, old fashioned steak! Remember the places in old New York back before everything went bust? Remember the champagne cocktails and the English mutton-chops you used to get at the Cheshire Cheese, with Yorkshire pudding on the side and brandy with the coffee? Remember the inch-thick steaks served sizzling at O. Henry's in the Village? For that matter, I'd sell what's left of my soul for one of those cheapy $1.29 steak dinners I used to get at Tad's on 42nd Street when I was low on the cash.

I'll be crying like a baby in a minute. *Think.* Use the brain or you'll end up in Cloud-Cuckoo-Land for sure. Cloud-Cuckoo-Land. "Nephelococcygia" in the original Greek, from *The Birds*, a comedy by Aristophones, a satirical caricature of Athenian politics—"4th century B.C. Athens in feathers," as somebody once called it.

My chances of being discovered are one in a million. Sure, the powerpack that keeps my airsuit life-support systems running radiates all over the spectrum . . . sure, any passing ship would detect that power-source . . . but who gives a damn? Who would even notice that feeble flicker on the detectors before they were a quarter of a light year beyond me, traveling fast? If my emergency deleo beacon were operable somebody might catch and even pause to investigate the automatic mayday signal, repeated over and over and . . . naw, what's the good of trying to fool myself? . . . I'm too far off the lanes for a rescue . . . and anything traveling way out here would be in paraspace anyway, with all detectors shut down . . .

I should just give up. Give up and die. Admit I'm beat, and face it like a man. My hand is on the release switch right now. One twist and my faceplate is open and I am dead. Nothing to fear . . . nothing to feel . . . I'll be stone dead before my blood boils or my eyeballs rupture or my lungs explode . . . dead and drifting alone forever between the silent cold mocking glitter of the stars. . . .

SIXTEEN

Again my consciousness dimmed and I swam for a time through numb colorless mists, devoid of identity, without sensation or awareness or even thought.

Loud voices impinged upon my drifting consciousness.

The voices rang with urgency and alarm. But I was unmoved, placid, unresponding. The words merely registered on the surface of my mind as I rose slowly towards awareness.

First a girl's voice, a young vibrant voice, but curiously flat and toneless, as if wrung tense under the pressure of some intolerable emotional strain . . .

"Stop it. Stop it. You are killing him. Stop it."

Then an older woman's voice, shrill with surprise—the urgency in her words sharp enough to pierce the dull fog of indifference that blurred my mind. . . .

"*Meade?* Where did you get that. . . ."

"Stop it. Get away from him. He has suffered enough."

Then the other voice again, shrillness of surprise gone now, very careful and quiet but full of tension. The sort of carefully colorless voice you use when speaking to a madman suddenly free, and armed, and dangerous.

"Meade. Dear. This is grandmother. Listen to me, darling. Put down the gun. Do you understand? The gun. Put it down."

"No. I won't. Leave him alone! You've hurt him enough!"

Then a third voice, rasping and cold, hoarse with strain, in a low rush of frantic words. . . .

159

"Her mind . . . I can't reach it . . . she has a mindlock. . . ."

"A *mindlock?*"

And the girl's voice again, still dull and toneless but colored a little with mischievous, sly humor—like the voice of a child, a child misbehaving, and knowing it, and enjoying it.

"Your mindlock, grandmother, your special mindlock. The one you wear so the ugly thing in the chair can't snoop on you. Now leave him alone!"

"Do what she says—quickly—I cannot control her when she is in this mood!" A terse whisper, choked with rage and rather surprisingly, with fear.

Then the faint touch of a smooth warm young hand, hesitantly, on my face. I could feel it, but at a distance, remotely. As if my nerves were wrapped in cotton batting.

"He's dead. *You killed him!*"

The rasping voice, dry and croaking with suppressed fear. . . .

"No, no, girl! He's alive. Drugged, that's all. I swear it! A harmless drug to make his mind sleep!"

"Make him wake up. *Now!*"

The woman's voice again, controlled, gentle, sweetly reasonable.

"Meade, dear, you must be a good girl or grandmother will be angry, very angry. Now, you don't want grandmother to be angry with you, darling! Just give grandmother the gun . . . *now!*"

"No. I hate you. You are a mean old woman. Make him wake up!"

A terse whisper . . . "She means it, she'll use the gun! Quick, give him the counteractive, you fool!" . . . and then I felt the cold nozzle of a hypospray against my skin and the tingle of the jet as it painlessly penetrated my flesh. And then everything went numb and vague for awhile, and suddenly I was wide awake. Wide awake and alert, with my mind crystal clear, and in full possession of all my faculties. The restorative worked superbly but all it could do was to clear my head. My skull felt like a throbbing drum and my brain was afire. I had the Imperator of all headaches. I focussed my eyes and peered blearily around.

I had been stripped and tied down on a metal table. Trays of medical instruments were set all about the table, bottles of drugs stood in neat racks and concealed lighting flooded the room with a sourceless, shadowless glow. It looked like a miniature operating theatre but I wasn't fooled. I had seen interrogation laboratories before, and this was one.

The straps were loosened and I sat up. Or tried to. I closed my teeth down, choking back a groan. I felt as if I had been beaten all over with padded truncheons. Every movement sent a stabbing needle of red pain ripping through me. But it was all right— the dampener had been shut off at last, and I used my mental control of my involuntary nervous system to block out the pain. The lancing agony in my muscles and the intolerable headache faded away mercifully. I looked around.

Across the room what was left of the crippled Star lay black and twisted in the wreckage of its chair. The stench of charred flesh was thick in the air and the hand-laser lay on the floor where Meade had dropped it. The girl lay in a crumpled heap by the table, sobbing in great racking heaves, her thin shoulders shaking. She must have turned the laser on the screaming thing in the chair and held the trigger down, spraying the telepath with the beam as if she had been using a hose to water the roses. It was very, very dead.

I staggered to my feet and looked around for the old woman, but she was not there. She must have fled

161

while Meade was roasting her pet telepath. That meant we had to move quickly. Madame Lyntonhurst would have her security forces on us in no time.

I felt no pain, only numbness. Red marks were cut deep across my upper chest, arms, belly and thighs. Under interrogation I must have fought against the restraining straps. I felt utterely exhausted from the ordeal and the first thing I did was to fumble with numb fingers among the racks of pharmaceuticals, peering bearily at labels. I selected a tube of stiminol-24, fumbled it into the receptor chamber of the hypospray, and held the jet against an artery. I shot enough gunk into my system to put a cadaver back into action and I felt it take hold almost immediately. My senses sharpened, the numbness and dull fatigue vanished, my limbs steadied and I felt ready to cope again.

The dose was dangerously massive but at least it put me back on my feet again, with enough go-power (I hoped) to get out of this place on my own. I had enough stiminol to keep me going for hours, and in fighting condition.

I would pay for it later, of course. I would be flat on my back and weak as a kitten for days. But that worry I left for later, remembering the old *haiku* poet, Okuma Kotomichi—

> *I will enjoy today*
> *Drinking whatever wine I have today.*
> *Tomorrow's sorrow*
> *I will endure tomorrow.*

—Which were my sentiments exactly.

Meade was a mass of jangled nerves and tears and hysteria from sheer reaction, so I gave her a shot of gunk as well. This was probably the first time in her

162

miserable, brow-beaten life she had ever openly defied the old woman to so drastic an extent and the wrench of the effort had used just about all of the guts the poor kid had been able to muster. But I knew a stiff jolt of stiminol would put some starch back into her spine quickly enough.

She lifted a pale, tear-wet face to me, lips trembling mutely. Her sweet girlish face was brutally swollen from the savage abuse she had supinely swallowed at the hands of her Grandmother. Just remembering that grisly scene back in the quiet, perfectly-decorated room—the tamed, will-less girl bending over so those cruel sharp fingernails could ravage her face—made my gorge rise. Meade had treated her lacerations and painted them over with the same quick-healing gel and cosmetic dye I had used on my abrasions back in the hotel suite on Demaratus. But the wan oval of her face was puffy and the bruises were purple welts, pitifully visible even through the dye.

I gave her shoulder a thank-you squeeze, and I grinned and made the thumbs-up salute that was probably too ancient for her to recognize.

"I had to do it," she quavered. "I just had to do it, Saul."

"I know you did, honey, and I thank you for it."

"They were *killing* you. It was awful. That ugly thing was hanging over you like a . . . like a big poisonous leech . . . whispering to you. . . ."

"Try to forget it now, kid. Pull yourself together. We've got to get out of here fast before Grandma sics the shock troops on us."

". . . Manipulating your *mind* . . . and you were twisting and fighting against the straps so terribly . . ." She shuddered and squeezed her eyes tight to block out the picture. I found my clothes tossed into a corner and climbed into them.

163

"Just forget it now, Meade. How do we get out of here, anyway?"

"That way," she pointed. "It opens into the hall."

"Which hall?" I asked, trying to remember the layout of the mansion. She told me and I visualized the situation: the gardens beyond the conservatory rooms —not too far to go before we could get out. I wanted to get out into the open fast. We'd have a better chance out there. Too many booby-traps could be built into these rooms and corridors. They could gas us through the air system and perhaps beam us down from remote-control guns concealed anywhere, in chandeliers, behind false wall panels, in doorways. All kinds of traps were possible in a place like this.

I had my clothes on by now, seamed up my boots and grabbed the laser she had let fall. Then I took her by the arm, pulled her to her feet and steered her towards the door. We had to pass near the charred thing in the broken chair and Meade shuddered and winced away from it.

"I had to do it," she whimpered. "After he used the hypo on you he tried to knock the laser out of my hand . . . I had to turn the gun on him!"

"Sure you did, baby. I understand. It's okay, don't worry about it. But what happened to your grandmother? Did you . . . ?"

She shivered.

"Oh, *no!* I just couldn't. I threatened to but I just *couldn't!* She must have gotten out when I was . . . while I shot the . . . I don't know! I looked around and she was gone!"

"Okay, don't worry about it. Come on. Keep behind me now and if I say jump—jump! Got that?"

She nodded, tremulous, big eyes solemn.

"Yes, Saul."

The corridor was brightly-lit and empty. We

164

closed the lab door behind us and went down the hall past any number of rooms into whose use and purpose I did not bother to inquire. This was the technical wing, I remember, fixing the positions of the files and commo and decoding complexes I had briefly explored before running into that robot.

Everything was quiet. Too damn quiet for my tastes! Why weren't the alarms going off and the halls flooding with guards, robotic or human? Why weren't the air conduits squirting gas at us? Surely, Madame Lyntonhurst had alerted her Control by now. Surely we were being monitored every inch of the way by spy rays. Surely the old witch didn't mean to let us escape?

Was she laying off the gunplay because Meade was with me? I grinned crookedly at the thought. Blood was thinner than water, I felt sure, where Madame Lyntonhurst was concerned. I knew her well enough to know that she would sacrifice her granddaughter without a single qualm. If by so doing she could get me under control. Besides, Meade was—must be—completely useless to her now. The kid had been manipulated and disciplined and tortured and psychologized, but she had more guts and more backbone than even Grandma ever realized. The worm had turned, the victim had struck back for once, and if I understood Madame Lyntonhurst as well as I thought I did, Meade was useless to her now. The tool was broken and had at last turned against the hand that had wielded it. It could never be fully trusted again, so Meade was marked for death as much as I was.

Down that corridor and into a branching one, past empty rooms and abandoned guard posts, we went, doubtless tripping every alarm in the system. My sensories were out to their fullest extent, searching, alert to danger. My mind was fixed on that gig parked out beyond the flower beds, if it was still there—the gig I had ridden down from the freighter's orbit, hours or days or weeks before—I had lost track of time under that hallucinogen.

Surely we wouldn't be allowed to reach the gig. And if we were, for some reason, permitted to get that far, surely there were laser batteries mounted on the roof of the mansion. Surely we'd be picked off before we got out of the atmosphere! They must have established standard operating procedures to cover emergency situations such as this one. Why, then, was nothing happening to block our escape? It was a real baffler. I didn't like it one bit and it was beginning to smell like a trap!

Then everything started to happen at once.

My sensories detected electrostatic tension snapping into force around us mere micro-seconds before the tangler-field closed us in its impalpable grip. Meade shrieked and struck out blindly against the eerie, molasses-like clutch and drag and cling of the tangler as it settled about us like instant quicksand. We were running at the moment the trap was sprung. The sudden drag against our legs tripped us and we toppled forward in one of those weird slow-motion falls. I grabbed for Meade and she clutched at me, yelling as our bodies drifted slowly—slowly—toward the floor.

Wall panels slid aside with a *snick*. Grinning guards stood in camouflaged niches lifting stunners towards us and I knew it was time to yell for help, so I yelled.

Now, Wanderer! Hit 'em hard!

My telepathic cry, boosted by the little gadget planted in the mastoid bone behind my ear, went winging into space, arrowing from the surface of the little terraformed planetoid to *Wanderer*'s orbit.

Ever since my capture that little self-powered gizmo behind my ear had been broadcasting its carrier wave even while I was asleep or drugged or otherwise non compos mentis—even while my mental activity was repressed by a dampener field, or my hallucinating brain was being probed by the twisted little monster in the hoverchair. Night and day, hour after hour, that indetectable carrier wave kept radiating its minute signal for the exclusive benefit of the waiting receptors of *Wanderer*'s thedominic brain.

Locked into alignment with that tiny pulsating signal, *Wanderer* had followed me every minute of time since I fell into that trap back at Demaratus Station. Constantly monitoring my wave, *Wanderer* had taken up its orbit around Madame Lyntonhurst's private planetoid estate and sat there waiting.

And when I yelled for help at last, my ship was ready. Shielded behind some of the most intricate and detector-proof fields and baffles ever designed, *Wanderer* had lurked in secrecy, its presence unsuspected all this while. Now it sprang into action with blinding speed.

The sky filled with light as the freighter, still in orbit above, was attacked without warning out of nowhere. Her energy screens flared before the force of intolerable beams. They fluoresced and went down, one by one. Before the dazzle of collapsing screens faded, a new brilliance blazed up as *Wanderer* raked the unshielded freighter from stem to stern with his primaries. The hull ruptured and came apart. Hull plates of collapsium-stressed steel crumpled and flared into roiling clouds of incandescent gas. Then one primary searched out and found the power center and it blew. The expanding fireball lit the surface of the little planetoid like a second sun.

Then *Wanderer* came down. Fast.

I could see none of this, of course, caught in the gluey grip if that tangler field. The foregoing, in fact, had taken place in slightly less than a tenth of a second and I was still falling forward slowly to the thick carpets. But I was *en rapport* with my ship and for the moment I "saw" through his detectors and "felt" through his screens, and time for me moved at the electronic swiftness of a thedominic spaceship's cogitative and neural reactions. And that is *fast!*

Planet-mounted laser batteries lifted into view from places of concealment in greenhouses, groves of trees, ornamental rooftop cupolas, gazebos and the like.

Wanderer appeared in the sky, a minute dead-black ovoid coming straight down. Air hissed about it and became superheated from friction. The hull glowed redly for a fraction of a second before the screens went up.

The black ovoid expanded with breath-taking speed until it became an immense, darkly metallic object filling the sky above the mansion. Its cylindrical shadow covered the lawn.

Super-swift laser batteries spouted needles of intolerable fire. *Wanderer*'s outer screens flared up, steadied, but held. I (mentally) grinned. *Wanderer*'s screens were receptors, not repulsors. The energy of attacking beams was diverted into banks of empty power cells. The screens soaked up all the power being poured into them, ran the same through the converters, and *stored* it! With this kind of a hook-up, *Wanderer*'s screens could absorb quite a lot of punishment without taking any harm!

Now he brought his secondaries into play. The ground shook, light flared blindingly and clouds of oily black smoke swirled up as his unerring beam knocked out the camouflaged laser batteries one by one.

Madame Lyntonhurst's planetoid estate was rigged out like a private fortress. But the major strength of her armaments was devoted to auto-guided missiles,

168

with the planet-mounted laser batteries serving only as a last-ditch line of defense, designed for close-up work to prevent troop carriers from landing. She had not been able to employ the main bulk of her defensive weaponry—the missiles—because *Wanderer* materialized well inside their zone of fire. It would have been a purely suicidal action to let those missiles, with their nucleonic warheads, attack a ship already well within the planetoid's artificial atmosphere. The fallout, even if the missiles were armed with "clean" warheads, to say nothing of the firestorm, would have scorched and scoured the surface of the planetoid clean of all life.

She had designed her defenses to cope with an assault force maneuvering in deep space. She had never planned on a sneak attack from inside her own defensive zone by a single ship.

Wanderer came down to a gentle planetfall. Tennis courts and gardens crunched to ruin, pulverized under the massive belly of the ship. He speared out with his secondaries, blindingly, and the Control center went up in a blaze with a deafening explosion. Marble facing, brickwork and structural ferroconcrete masonry, broken to rubble, came splattering down in a rocky rain of pebbles over several acres.

The whole front of one wing crumpled in and slid down in an avalanche of ruin. Marble fountains, statuary groups, garden walls of carven sciostone were crushed. From somewhere amidst the wreckage, water from a ruptured main fountained up and came down in a stinging hot shower.

The elapsed time from my mayday call to right now: one and one fifth seconds.

The power went off when Control blew up. Illuminants arced and died in a shower of sparks. The tangle-field snapped off just as Meade and I hit the

169

floor. I rolled over and came up, the laser-gun steady in my hand.

The guards were still frozen in shock from the suddenness of *Wanderer*'s devastating and thoroughly unexpected attack. My gun snapped off five shots and five men toppled from their camouflaged wall niches.

I bent and grabbed Meade's arm, pulling her to her feet.

"C'mon. We gotta get out of here *now*."

She lifted a stunned, bewildered face to me, "Wh-what—?"

"No time to jabber. *Move!*"

I propelled her across the room to the far side where tall French windows looked out on what had been a beautiful view of the gardens. Now flowering bushes lay broken and crushed under fallen bricks and white powdery ash; smouldering cinders coated the candle-wood trees and flower beds.

The window panes were of tough transparent plastic, of course, and not glass. They were still secure, instead of littering the floor with broken shards. I lifted the hand-laser and traversed from right to left firing a short burst. They exploded outward and I half-pushed, half-dragged the girl through their empty frames, slapping smouldering drapes aside. We jumped down to a ruined flower bed and I took a fast look around. Beyond a stand of blossoming trees *Wanderer* was visible, a glistening dark cylinder of metal.

"Over that way—come on!"

We sprinted for the safety of the ship. My heels dug deep in soft spongy loam as I ran. The air stank of burning wood, blistering enamel and rock-dust. It reeked with the sharp metallic stench of ozone from the gunfire.

Wanderer was snapping off quick shots. Picking

off pockets of resistance, I guess. Each short burst of fire lit the garden with dazzling unearthly light like a battery of old antique flashbulbs. For some inane reason I thought of the *paparazzi*, those old-time screwball Italian free-lance photographers popping their blinding flash-cameras in the faces of unwary celebrities. Funny what nutty memories and thoughts pop into your head when the heat's on and things are moving fast.

Meade squealed and went down in a patch of burnt flowers, her ankle turning in the mushy soil. I bent to help her and a bright beam went scorching across the lawn, zig-zagging towards us, digging a smouldering furrow through the dirt almost up to our feet. Somebody had gotten to the windows through which we had escaped only a moment before. Somebody with an energy weapon was trying to pick us off before we made it to the ship.

"DOWN!"

A mental command, deafening, crashed into my brain. I fell flat, dragging Meade down with me. A wave of intense heat passed above us as we lay grinding our faces into the mud. I felt the fabric crisp across my back and shoulders and the stinging heat bake in, raising welts and blisters in a sort of instant sunburn. Automatically, I threw up nerve-blocks. I was still running on the impetus of that shot of stiminol and was feeling no pain. Meade gasped from the blast of heat that travelled swiftly over us, but I was lying on top of her and took most of the punishment. The blinding glare of *Wanderer's* beam leaked through my tightly squeezed-shut eyes and the explosion behind us knocked the breath out of me. I felt the ground jump beneath our bodies. Dirt and pebbles rained thickly down. Something hit me on the shoulder. Something else—immeasurably bigger and heavier—

171

plowed into the earth directly in front of us, kicking a wave of hot mud over our heads and shoulders.

I got to my feet in a ringing silence, dirt and rubble pouring off me. Behind us, the whole side of the building had come apart and lay in smoking heaps of pulverized stone and splintered wood. I could hardly see, after-images of the beam's flash filling my field of vision with psychedelic kaleidoscopes of colored fire. And the explosion had deafened me—temporarily, I hoped.

It was quite a sight. Rags of expensive carpet hung from the denuded branches of one of the nearer candlewood trees. A smashed diorite bust had plowed like a cannonball through the seared turf of the lawn beyond the wrecked garden, digging up a raw ditch through dead grass. A freak effect of the blast had thrust a blackened oak beam into the ash-blanketed lawn, half-burying it. A few yards closer and it would have pulped us.

The great house was on fire now in a dozen places. One entire facade had slid into piles of rubble, laying three stories of wrecked rooms exposed to the view. There were a lot of bodies strewn about but none of them were moving. One ornamental chimney, a three-story-high tube of ceramic brick, had fallen, virtually in one piece—it stretched across the ash-whitened lawn like a low wall tumbled by an earthquake. Halfway down its meandering length it had crushed to earth two guards in a skimmer.

Our ears still ringing, we picked our way through the junk to *Wanderer*.

Halfway there we came upon another victim of the battle. A wall had burst outwards, spewing bricks for half a hundred yards in a deadly rain. That rain had caught and battered to death a fleeing form now unrecognizable and buried under a mound of broken brick. But the hand that stretched from beneath the heap of wreckage as if clawing for freedom—that hand was recognizable. Still slim, elegant and patrician, although dirtied now with ash and cinders and coarse brick-dust. And still wearing that iridium ring set with an immense Kyrian stardrop of flawless water.

Had Madame Lyntonhurst been fleeing to some place of concealment, some hidden refuge or secret avenue of escape, when that exploding hail of bricks had caught and crushed her plans of usurpation and conquest forever? Or had she merely been running from the ruined house in purposeless and panic-stricken flight? We would probably never know. . . .

I had my arm around Meade's shoulders, so I gave her a hug as she stared down silent, wide-eyed and white-faced at the unmoving thing crushed under a ton of fallen bricks.

She turned away without saying a word and went unsteadily across the wreckage-strewn lawn to where *Wanderer* lay, belly sunk deep in the turf, still snapping off shots to cover our approach, spacedoors yawning open to receive us.

The girl had not a word or a tear for the crushed thing under the bricks that had been her Grandmother. But I paused for just a moment to make a sketchy salute.

Ave et vale, I said in silent farewell to a worthy opponent.

SEVENTEEN

Later, months later, in fact—for you just don't walk away from a messy thing like a major conspiracy—you hang around and see that it gets cleaned up; and that takes time and lots of detail work. When you nip a conspiracy of this size in the bud, so to speak, it's not enough to just cut off its head. Too many lower-echelon members might get ambitions to assume command of whatever is left of the organizational structure. So you have to root it out cell by cell, branch by branch.

This job I turned over to Citadel. Partly through laziness and partly because the punishment, mental and physical, I had absorbed during those grueling hours of drugged interrogation left me stuck in a hospital for the better part of the following month. Citadel made a good job of it and, of course, Meade was an enormous help. As the only heir to her Grandmother's immense fortune *and* political organization, her whole-hearted cooperation made Citadel's job lots easier. Finally, of course, the complicated, ugly mess was cleaned up. Citadel does these things very smoothly—a secret underground organization itself—it doesn't have to worry about things like search warrants, *habeas corpus*, due process, courts or the lot.

Assassination is the cleanest way of getting rid of the Very Important Persons who were high up in the command structure of the Lyntonhurst conspiracy. And over the millennia, Citadel has raised the technique of unobtrusive deaths from natural causes, so-called, to the dignity of a fine art. Thus, for the ensuing

175

several months there was the most appalling mortality rate among the leading statesmen of the Imperium. They died like flies in all sorts of accidents and from a variety of hard-to-detect-in-advance ailments—planetary governors, Naval command personnel, local cluster-level political leaders, Ministry officials and even a few high-placed members of the Centumvirate, not to mention any number of hegemons and gentles of the lesser nobility. But finally it was all over.

The following is a transcribed account of a telepathic conversation some months afterwards. Since telepathic communication is essentially non-verbal, this transcription is woefully inadequate. But it conveys enough to pass muster.)

Hi, Meade! How's my girl? Keeping busy?
—*Saul?* (Incredulously.) *I'm just fine. But how are* YOU?
Back in one piece again: fit for basket-weaving, minor ceramics and similar forms of occupational therapy.
—*That's wonderful! I came to see you once when I had some time between trips* (picture of harried Meade with busy schedule on enormous clipboard in waiting room of noisy terminal full of flashing signs) *but you were under heavy sedation and I couldn't get in to see you.*
Yeah. (Comic groan and pained expression.) That must have been the time they spent nineteen hours picking pieces of busted brick out of my backside. But how do you like Citadel? They been keeping you busy?
—*Have they EVER!* (Picture of Meade, frowning, sweating, dishevelled, at desk covered with top secret memos, trying to answer fifteen videophone calls at once.) *But I like it: I feel useful, Saul, really USEFUL, for once. . . .*

So I gather, honey. I understand you are staying in Citadel for good, even though your part in smashing the conspiracy is about over. (Lifted eyebrows.) How come? Why the lady freedom-fighter stuff, instead of the lady of leisure—or have you forgotten just how RICH you are these days?

—*No, Saul, I haven't forgotten. My . . . my grandmother left me an incredible fortune but I also haven't forgotten just where all that money came from. You know we uncovered a lot of dirty business once we really started digging into the Party's records. . . .*

Huh? I thought she married the units. All those rich husbands—(a baffled shrug; "please elucidate".)

—*Not ALL of the units, not by a long shot. Oh, Saul, revolutions cost a lot these days, even underground ones. She had a finger in every filthy corner in the whole quadrant: vice, blackmail, illicit drugs, graft, crooked unions, kidnapping—the works! How could I live the life of leisure, knowing the human misery that paid for all my pretty things? Nope. Soon as I can fix the details, Citadel gets my fortune. They can put it to good use. . . .*

(Soberly.) Bless you for that, Meade.

—*(Awkward pause, then, wistfully:) I guess you're going home now. Saul? Am I ever going to . . . to see you again?*

Sure you will, honey! But not for some time, I'm afraid. Maybe a long time, I dunno. You've got lots to do, and me . . . well, I got a few things to clean up first. But just as soon as they're out of the way . . . !

—*(Wistfully.) Really, Saul? . . . Promise?*

Promise, baby. One of these days, I'll be back in your life to muck it up all over again. Till then, Meade: the best! (Picture of a goodbye kiss.)

—*The VERY best, Saul. Saul!*

Yeah, baby?

177

—Make it soon?

Soon. Sooner than you think, if everything goes right. And I know it will . . .

(END of transcription.)

AND SO I came home again. *Wanderer* came down gently as a falling leaf in the back pasture and I climbed out and stood for a moment watching my sun setting over the hills, just feeling the peace and quiet and breathing in the good clean air of Home.

And the dogs came whooping and hollering out to say hello. They aren't supposed to be allowed beyond the fence, but homecoming is a special time and the House relented for once and did not turn them back.

They came pouring through the fence, ecstatic and wriggling, tails lashing the long grasses in an hysteria of sheer joy. The two dachsies were in the lead and went gamboling around my feet yapping in a frenzy. I bent down and ruffled the fur behind their ears in the very special way they loved. Then my big St. Bernard boy came up, woofing his hellos. He stood up with his great paws set against my shoulders, his breath warm against my face, and licked me, letting me know everything was all right.

Even the puppies came out to say hello. I was not really very surprised, and even just a little bit sad, to see they were puppies no longer, but half grown dogs. They did not remember me at all, but something about my smell must have sounded a dim chord of memory in their doggy brains because they let me stroke them and admire how they had grown, and one of them, the fattest, even licked my fingers.

They gave me a yelping, prancing escort as I went through the pasture fence and into the yard. The long low house looked just the same as ever, redwood log and fieldstone and slate roof all very warm and cosy and familiar in the rich redgold haze of an autumn sunset. The tall maples were shedding their leaves and the wild rose bushes were bare and skeletal. The House had cut the lawn and trimmed the flower beds and had been raking up the fallen leaves, I saw, that very afternoon.

Wanderer knew how to let himself into the big red barn that served as his hangar, so I could safely leave the task to him. From within the barn I could hear Sultan thumping and neighing. He knew something had happened, and probably suspected I had come home. I made a mental promise to visit him before he bedded down. And I wanted to bring him an apple for a treat. Perhaps tomorrow morning I'd saddle him and take a long ride down by the shore. . . .

I went in and tossed my knap behind the door, looking around at the big, low-ceiling room I loved. A bright fire was crackling on the grate of the big fieldstone fireplace, its wavering glow painting the exposed beams of the ceiling with orange light. I looked around at the beer steins on the slate mantle, the antique swords and old guns on the oak panelled walls, and knew that I had come home.

"Welcome home, sir," the house said. "There have been no urgent messages, but a digest of current news is ready for your attention—"

"I'll look it over later," I grunted. "Right now I want a hot bath, a long massage and a vodka martini —a stiff one."

"At once, sir. The dogs have *not* been very good during your absence. There have been two fights and Molly was rather severely bitten on the left buttock, requiring three stitches . . ."

"I'll take the casualty report later, too," I said. "She looked lively enough when she came howling out to say hello."

179

"Yes, sir. Have you had your dinner, sir?"

"No, I haven't, and I'm glad you mentioned it. I'll have the thickest steak you've got, and a bottle of that Medoc if we still have any. But first a hot soak—and where's that martini?"

Two hours later, bathed, shaved, massaged, fed and half asleep, wrapped in an old robe and stretched out in my big comfortable chair, staring into the fire and listening to the wind howl around the eaves, I nursed a cigarette and a mug of steaming coffee and let my mind drift.

I would never see Meade again, and I think she knew it, but of course she didn't know why. Unless she had researched me in Citadel records and knew that I am an immortal, and is smart enough to put a few things together.

There's one aspect of immortality people never seem to think of, and that's *love*.

No immortal dare permit himself to love. *I* know.

I do not know, and I have not ever been able to find out, how I became an immortal. Whether from some one-in-ninety-billion accidents of genetics—some incredibly rare and elusive gene—or some freak mutation, never again repeated. I simply do not know how it happened.

And, not knowing how it happened, I cannot repeat it.

I am Earth's only immortal man and I am lonely.

And I dare not fall in love. For I can think of no more hideous fate than to go on ever young from year to year, watching the woman I loved and married grow old down the path of human mortality which I can never follow. That life would be a living hell, for me and for the woman I made my wife.

I could fall in love with Meade very easily.

180

That's why I must never see her again.

Night had fallen while I sat musing on the fire. Rain is lashing against the panes and it drums against the roof.

One of the dachsunds, Molly, the one with the half-healed bite in the behind, has wriggled up into my lap. She doesn't like rain, or thunder and lightning, for that matter, but if she is close to me she feels safe.

The big St. Bernard, Sir Dennis Nayland Smith, has settled down beside my chair with a long heavy sigh and gone to sleep.

My cigarette has gone out and my coffee is cold. I want another cigarette and another hot mug but I can't disturb the fat little dachsie snoring on my lap, so I just sit and stare sleepily into the dying fire.

It is good to be home.

Tomorrow I think I will take the yawl out for a sail down the coast if the wind is strong.

I must remember to tell the house I want a good spanking breeze and a bright sunny day for tomorrow.

THE END

CHRONOLOGY OF KEY HISTORICAL EVENTS MENTIONED IN THIS NOVEL

Anno Domini	Year of the Imperium	Description
2551		Rebellion of the Fourth Fleet; Battle of Phi Micae; PSEUDO-DEATH OF SAUL EVEREST; collapse of the United Systems.
2553		Murder of Gorem Chayce; the Hub Stars capitulate; Nordonn Korvys assumes dictatorial powers; formation of The Galactic State (i.e., "the Nordonnate").
3013		Saul Everest emerges from the race in the 462nd year since the Pseudodeath; formation of the Wolfpack.
3063	The Year One of the Imperium	As "Mikal Arion," Saul Everest assumes power following the demise of Nordonn XVII. The Nordonnate is abolished, and Mikal Arion begins his empery as the Imperator Arion I; THE FOUNDING OF THE GREAT IMPERIUM.
(3112)	49	"Death" of Arion I; empery of Ralric begins; CITADEL IS ESTABLISHED IN SECRET BY SAUL EVEREST.
(3468)	407	Period of the novel, *The Man Without a Planet*, which takes place in the fifth year of Arban IV, Imperator of the House of Tridian.
(7015)	3962	Saul Everest "retires" from active participation in Citadel activities.
(7177)	4114	Period of the novel, *Star Rogue*, which takes place in the twenty-seventh year of Kermian XIX, Imperator of the House of Tregephon.

AUTHOR'S NOTE

In a very real sense, any novel laid in the extremely distant future (such as this one) must be regarded as a translation. And, as a translation, in common with all other translations, it must fail.

In another sense, such a novel also partakes of the basic nature of prophecy. And, again in common with all other specimens of its kind, it is foredoomed to failure. By this I mean that while a prophecy may succeed in broad outline, it is certainly going to fail in the details and particulars of the events or developments it strives to predict.

(A note on this matter of prophecy. There are two kinds: the wild guess, and the informed speculation. Oddly enough, the informed speculation usually flops dismally—*viz.* all the "atomic doom" stories popular in *Astounding Science Fiction* in the years immediately following the close of the Second World War. Uniformly, they predicted an atomic holocaust coming in the next twenty years—say by 1966 at latest—but WWIII has yet to occur, for which I thank the Plenum. Those stories were concocted by engineers and social scientists, yet while they succeeded in extrapolating political tensions visible in their time, as well as the rapid growth of nuclear technology to the degree of expertise needed to make an atomic war a real Armageddon, they failed to predict that nations as dissimilar as the U.S. and the U.S.S.R. would somehow learn to live with each other and both with the fact of The Bomb.

(But the wild guess often comes uncannily close.

Like Dean Swift. In *Gulliver* he made an incredibly precise guess as to the number, relative size, and even the orbits of the moons of Mars . . . no less than one hundred and fifty-one years before Asaph Hall actually discovered them. Or "Ol' World-Wrecker" himself, Edmond Hamilton. Way back in 1942 in one of his marvelous Captain Future yarns he predicted that man would reach the moon by 1971. He was only two years off. Pretty accurate for a guess made twenty-seven years before the event; especially remarkable when you consider that it was the vast advance in technology spurred by World War II that made it possible for Neil Armstrong to take his giant leap so soon.)

But back to the matter of viewing a novel of the distant future as a translation.

Star Rogue is set in the Year 4114 of the Imperium, which works out to A.D. 7177 according to my private fictional chronology. In other words, the scenery of the novel is laid 5207 years from now. It is literally impossible for any author—not just Lin Carter, but *anybody*—to make a guess at the living conditions fifty-two centuries ahead with anything like the remotest accuracy. You could convene a congress of the most erudite and imaginative philosophers, sociologists, technologists and speculative historians, pose the question of what life will be like fifty-two centuries from now, collate the results—and you'll come up with a composite picture that is almost certain to be at least 70% dead wrong, at a conservative estimate.

This is because you just cannot predict the unpredictable. And history is made up of unpredictables.

Look at what life was like A.D. 470, which is only fifteen centuries back. Men wore robes, togas, buskins, tunics. They drank watered wine and had two

186

meals a day. They served an absolute monarchy or an autocratic empire with a rigid class system. Save for a couple of hair-brained philosophers, they were certain their world was the center of the universe and probably flat as a pancake. They were merchants, or noblemen, or warriors, or statesmen, or farm laborers. They worshipped either official State pantheons or exotic cults imported from the East. They were middle-aged at forty and senile at sixty, if they lived that long. They believed in magic and astrology and most of them were of the opinion that disease was the work of malignant spirits.

Today—only fifteen centuries later—we wear business suits, ties, jackets, sweaters. We drink coffee and cocktails, smoke tobacco, eat fresh meat and fruit flown half a continent to our table. We live in a social system devoid, to a very large extent, of hereditary privilege and divided largely on by economic lines alone, and managed for us by elected officials chosen to represent geo–political divisions. We comprehend and use the germ theory of disease, are not middle aged until about sixty (and some of us, like Cary Grant and Loretta Young, just *never* get middle-aged) and die of old age in our eighties, unless cut down earlier by one or another of the very few diseases we have not yet conquered. We are tradesmen, manufacturers, scientists, artists, clerical or executive workers, municipal employees or factory technicians. We pay lip-service to one or another schismatic fragment of a once-worldwide religion but mostly we think for ourselves without the thought-control of official dogma. We have explored, mapped, colonized and tamed the entire globe and are currently engaged in performing the same task throughout the rest of our planetary system.

And these are only the superficial changes reflected

on the surface of daily living. Yet most of them are
due to those little unpredictables that, by very definition, cannot be foreseen. Before the Conquistadores,
who could guess that the South American continent
would divulge new substances—like rubber, coffee,
chocolate—which would change human living patterns? Before the Bastille fell, who could predict that
the cruel excesses of hereditary privilege would produce, in reaction, a classless, self-governing society
from which (once the profit-incentive of capitalism
was added to it) would spring a wave of technological innovation—telephone, radio, automobile, air-
plane, electric light—the influence of which would
be incalculable?

How, then, can any author—even a Heinlein, an
Asimov or a Clarke—make anything like an informed
guess at the alterations to be introduced in human
society during the next few thousand years? Very
simply, they can't.

For those readers who are interested in this sort of
thing, this novel is one of a sequence of novels, connected only by a continuing background history, to
which I have given the overall title of *History of the
Great Imperium*. I now visualize this sequence as con-
sisting eventually of at least eight, and perhaps as
many as twelve, component novels. The only novel
in the History yet published is my *The Man Without
a Planet* (1966), which was set in the fifth year of
the empery of Arban IV, of the House of Tridian, in
Year 407 of the Imperium (A.D. 3468), or 3709 years
before this book, *Star Rogue*.

As now planned, there will be a gap of centuries,
even millennia, between the component novels. Naturally, there will be no overlap of characters—Saul
Everest will appear but rarely—and, of course, each

novel will or should stand on its own as an individual story which the reader can enjoy and understand without it being necessary that he read all of the other novels in the sequence.

Keeping all of the foregoing points in mind, you will see that the social and technological innovations in *Star Rogue* are not intended to be serious predictions of Things To Come. But they *are* designed to represent the *fact* that major and basic changes in human life will occur over such immense spans of time. My concepts are meant to stand as a sort of shorthand for unpredictable changes to come. It is short-sighted to assume that anything resembling the representational elective government of mid-20th Century America will survive in a galactic society fifty-two hundred years hence: thus my "Imperium" (the term, less familiar than "empire" but obviously related to it, was selected to stand for "something kind of like an empire"), tempered by the influence of a Centumvirate ("something kind of like a parliament, crossed with a council of lobbyists representing the special interests of powerful groups and factions"). It is even more short-sighted to assume that we will still be using such gadgets as radio or television or radar or IBM computers, at least as we now know them. Hence my "deleo" and "asdar" and "thedomin" whose uses are clearly obvious from the context of the story.

And I assume the distant future, with a different kind of society, will speak a different language (hence my "Neoanglic," as different from today's English as Norman Mailer is from Chaucer; use different slang terms ("proctor" for "policeman"); and have different modes of address ("Cn. and Cns." for "Mr. and Miss"). What these terms *will* be I have no way

189

of knowing. My easy, obvious and not really very original terms are only there to remind you of the fact that there *will* be new terms.

I have made the average life-expectancy two hundred plus, added telepathy as a new fact of the human condition, and, for good measure, tossed in a couple of new religions (Vuudhana and Plenumolatry). None of this need be taken very seriously.

In fact, you can be certain of only one thing about life in A.D. 7177. It will be totally different in every way from anything Anderson, Blish, Carter, de Camp, Ellison, Farmer, Garrett, Heinlein, Jakes, Kuttner, Laumer, Moorcock, Niven, Oliver, Pohl, Russell, Simak, Tenn, Van Vogt, Williamson, or Zelazny ever dared to dream.

And that *is* a certainty!

—LIN CARTER

Hollis, Long Island, New York.

THE END

www.ingramcontent.com/pod-product-compliance
Lightning Source LLC
Chambersburg PA
CBHW032009240626
47153CB00003B/1188